DANGER IN THE DESERT

As Malva opened the door of her cabin, she then hesitated for a moment wondering whether she should ask Royden to release the trapped bird instead of going on deck herself.

Then she told herself that he would be fast asleep and it would be unnecessary to wake him, especially as she herself was now so awake.

She moved slowly towards the companionway and walked out on deck without making a sound.

There was, she knew, usually a seaman on duty, but she had suspected long ago that when they were in Port he slept because it was so quiet.

Her cabin was halfway along the deck and she had no difficulty in finding it from above and then leant over the rail.

She saw the bird fluttering frantically beneath her.

As she looked down, she could see that its leg was attached quite firmly to the side of the porthole.

She knelt down and bent forward to cut him loose with her pair of scissors.

As she did so, a heavy cloth was thrown over her head and she was lifted up from the deck.

A strong man was holding her in his arms.

THE BARBARA CARTLAND PINK COLLECTION

Titles in this series

1. The Cross Of Love
2. Love In The Highlands
3. Love Finds The Way
4. The Castle Of Love
5. Love Is Triumphant
6. Stars In The Sky
7. The Ship Of Love
8. A Dangerous Disguise
9. Love Became Theirs
10. Love Drives In
11. Sailing To Love
12. The Star Of Love
13. Music Is The Soul Of Love
14. Love In The East
15. Theirs To Eternity
16. A Paradise On Earth
17. Love Wins In Berlin
18. In Search Of Love
19. Love Rescues Rosanna
20. A Heart In Heaven
21. The House Of Happiness
22. Royalty Defeated By Love
23. The White Witch
24. They Sought Love
25. Love Is The Reason For Living
26. They Found Their Way To Heaven
27. Learning To Love
28. Journey To Happiness
29. A Kiss In The Desert
30. The Heart Of Love
31. The Richness Of Love
32. For Ever And Ever
33. An Unexpected Love
34. Saved By An Angel
35. Touching The Stars
36. Seeking Love
37. Journey To Love
38. The Importance Of Love
39. Love By The Lake
40. A Dream Come True
41. The King Without A Heart
42. The Waters Of Love
43. Danger To The Duke
44. A Perfect Way To Heaven
45. Follow Your Heart
46. In Hiding
47. Rivals For Love
48. A Kiss From The Heart
49. Lovers In London
50. This Way To Heaven
51. A Princess Prays
52. Mine For Ever
53. The Earl's Revenge
54. Love At The Tower
55. Ruled By Love
56. Love Came From Heaven
57. Love And Apollo
58. The Keys Of Love
59. A Castle Of Dreams
60. A Battle Of Brains
61. A Change Of Hearts
62. It Is Love
63. The Triumph Of Love
64. Wanted – A Royal Wife
65. A Kiss Of Love
66. To Heaven With Love
67. Pray For Love
68. The Marquis Is Trapped
69. Hide And Seek For Love
70. Hiding From Love
71. A Teacher Of Love
72. Money Or Love
73. The Revelation Is Love
74. The Tree Of Love
75. The Magnificent Marquis
76. The Castle
77. The Gates Of Paradise
78. A Lucky Star
79. A Heaven On Earth
80. The Healing Hand
81. A Virgin Bride
82. The Trail To Love
83. A Royal Love Match
84. A Steeplechase For Love
85. Love At Last
86. Search For A Wife
87. Secret Love
88. A Miracle Of Love
89. Love And The Clans
90. A Shooting Star
91. The Winning Post Is Love
92. They Touched Heaven
93. The Mountain Of Love
94. The Queen Wins
95. Love And The Gods
96. Joined By Love
97. The Duke Is Deceived
98. A Prayer For Love
99. Love Conquers War
100. A Rose In Jeopardy
101. A Call Of Love
102. A Flight To Heaven
103. She Wanted Love
104. A Heart Finds Love
105. A Sacrifice For Love
106. Love's Dream In Peril
107. Soft, Sweet And Gentle
108. An Archangel Called Ivan
109. A Prisoner In Paris
110. Danger In The Desert

DANGER IN THE DESERT

BARBARA CARTLAND

bc.com

Barbaracartland.com Ltd

Copyright © 2013 by Cartland Promotions
First published on the internet in November 2013
by Barbaracartland.com Ltd

ISBN 978-1-78213-434-3

The characters and situations in this book are entirely imaginary and bear no relation to any real person or actual happening.

This book is sold subject to the condition that it shall not, by way of trade or otherwise, be lent, resold, hired out or otherwise circulated without the publisher's prior consent. No part of this publication may be reproduced or transmitted in any form or by any means, electronically or mechanically, including photocopying, recording or any information storage or retrieval, without the prior permission in writing from the publisher.

Printed and bound in Great Britain
by Mimeo of Huntingdon, Cambridgeshire.

THE BARBARA CARTLAND PINK COLLECTION

Dame Barbara Cartland is still regarded as the most prolific bestselling author in the history of the world.

In her lifetime she was frequently in the Guinness Book of Records for writing more books than any other living author.

Her most amazing literary feat was to double her output from 10 books a year to over 20 books a year when she was 77 to meet the huge demand.

She went on writing continuously at this rate for 20 years and wrote her very last book at the age of 97, thus completing an incredible 400 books between the ages of 77 and 97.

Her publishers finally could not keep up with this phenomenal output, so at her death in 2000 she left behind an amazing 160 unpublished manuscripts, something that no other author has ever achieved.

Barbara's son, Ian McCorquodale, together with his daughter Iona, felt that it was their sacred duty to publish all these titles for Barbara's millions of admirers all over the world who so love her wonderful romances.

So in 2004 they started publishing the 160 brand new Barbara Cartlands as *The Barbara Cartland Pink Collection*, as Barbara's favourite colour was always pink – and yet more pink!

The Barbara Cartland Pink Collection is published monthly exclusively by Barbaracartland.com and the books are numbered in sequence from 1 to 160.

Enjoy receiving a brand new Barbara Cartland book each month by taking out an annual subscription to the Pink Collection, or purchase the books individually.

The Pink Collection is available from the Barbara Cartland website www.barbaracartland.com via mail order and through all good bookshops.

In addition Ian and Iona are proud to announce that The Barbara Cartland Pink Collection is now available in ebook format as from Valentine's Day 2011.

For more information, please contact us at:

Barbaracartland.com Ltd.
Camfield Place
Hatfield
Hertfordshire AL9 6JE
United Kingdom

Telephone: +44 (0)1707 642629
Fax: +44 (0)1707 663041
Email: info@barbaracartland.com

THE LATE DAME BARBARA CARTLAND

Barbara Cartland who sadly died in May 2000 at the age of nearly 99 was the world's most famous romantic novelist who wrote 723 books in her lifetime with worldwide sales of over 1 billion copies and her books were translated into 36 different languages.

As well as romantic novels, she wrote historical biographies, 6 autobiographies, theatrical plays, books of advice on life, love, vitamins and cookery. She also found time to be a political speaker and television and radio personality.

She wrote her first book at the age of 21 and this was called *Jigsaw*. It became an immediate bestseller and sold 100,000 copies in hardback and was translated into 6 different languages. She wrote continuously throughout her life, writing bestsellers for an astonishing 76 years. Her books have always been immensely popular in the United States, where in 1976 her current books were at numbers 1 & 2 in the B. Dalton bestsellers list, a feat never achieved before or since by any author.

Barbara Cartland became a legend in her own lifetime and will be best remembered for her wonderful romantic novels, so loved by her millions of readers throughout the world.

Her books will always be treasured for their moral message, her pure and innocent heroines, her good looking and dashing heroes and above all her belief that the power of love is more important than anything else in everyone's life.

"Love is so beautiful that the glory of the Himalayas and the majesty of the Taj Mahal come nowhere near its perfection."

Barbara Cartland

CHAPTER ONE
1870

The Earl of Hillingwood climbed out of his carriage outside White's Club in St. James's Street and walked up the steps.

The Club porter was standing by the door and he bowed politely and greeted him,

"Good morning, your Lordship, it's very nice to see you back at the Club."

"I am very delighted to be here, Jasper," the Earl replied. "London seems at its best this time of the year."

He did not wait for the porter to say anything more, but walked straight into the coffee room.

As it was fairly early in the day, there were only a few members sitting around talking to each other.

The Earl walked almost to the far end of the room where he found his habitual seat and then settled himself comfortably into it.

He had not been there for more than a few minutes when he was joined by his old friend, Lord Waverstone, who called out as he reached him,

"You are always over-punctual, Edward, and now you will tell me I am late!"

The Earl laughed and countered,

"No, but, as you say, I am somewhat over-punctual and you are exactly on time!"

"I was wondering when I heard from you," Lord Waverstone said, "why you were coming to London when I am sure that your garden has never looked more beautiful in the spring and your horses are doubtless running faster than ever."

The Earl laughed again.

"I want to see you, Arthur" he began slowly, "on a matter that deeply concerns me and I think also concerns you."

Lord Waverstone looked surprised.

But he merely settled down in a seat next to his friend and signalled to a Steward.

When the man reached him, he ordered a large pot of coffee.

"You are very abstemious," the Earl remarked. "Is this a new departure?"

"No, it is only a precaution," his friend replied. "I have to go to a large luncheon party today and if I start drinking now I will undoubtedly feel ill this evening, when I have yet another party to attend."

The Earl smiled.

"You have always been the same, but I am quite certain that, if you are making a speech at both events, you will undoubtedly have to pay for what you eat and what you drink."

"That unfortunately is the truth," Lord Waverstone replied. "The trouble is that people today are too lazy to find other performers, so I am continually in demand!"

"Now you are being over-modest," the Earl chided. "You know as well as I do that no one speaks better than you in the House of Lords. As Queen Victoria said to me the other day, you have a presence which in her opinion most of the young men lack."

"I am delighted to accept the compliment. Now tell me, Edward, why you have asked me here to meet you? I have a feeling, although I am not sure, that something may well be wrong."

"Not wrong, but I have been considering for a long time, as I think you know, that it is absolutely essential that Royden, my one and only son and heir, should get married. So I have decided that you are the only person who can help me."

Lord Waverstone looked at him in bewilderment.

But he then merely asked of his old friend,

"In what way?"

As if he had not spoken, the Earl went on,

"Royden is now twenty-eight and, as I have pointed out continually, it is time he married and settled down and produced an heir, in fact several of them."

Lord Waverstone had heard this before.

"I know your feelings on this matter," he replied, "but Royden is a great success in the Social world and his *affaires-de-coeur* seldom last very long as he much prefers to move from beauty to beauty as if he was a honeybee."

He paused for a moment before he continued,

"The husbands go fishing or look the other way and Royden can then add another triumph to his considerable collection!"

There was a very distinct touch of humour in Lord Waverstone's voice as he spoke.

But the Earl did not even smile.

He only parried,

"Let me be frank with you, Arthur, I am not as well as I used to be and I am determined to make sure that my Family Tree does not end abruptly as it might easily do."

"My dear Edward, I am sure that you are talking nonsense," Lord Waverstone said. "You are a very healthy man and I can see no reason why you should not live for another twenty years at least."

The Earl shook his head.

"It's not as easy as that, I only wish it was. I have been told by the doctors to go steady and as you can guess that means no riding. I will also have to give up my yearly trips abroad which I always find so enjoyable."

"I am deeply sorry to hear that," Lord Waverstone answered, "I know how much you enjoy going to France and Switzerland. And I always thought that you came back better for the change of air and even a change of friends."

"I have no friend I can depend on in the same way as I depend on you" the Earl replied. "Therefore, Arthur, you must help me because what I want more than anything else concerns you as much as it concerns me."

Lord Waverstone raised one eyebrow.

But instead of asking questions, he suggested,

"Go on, Edward. You know I am listening."

For a moment there was silence.

And then the Earl said,

"I have begged Royden, almost on bended knee, to marry, but he merely tells me that there is plenty of time for that in the future and he finds young women boring, in fact he dislikes the whole idea of being married."

As Lord Waverstone knew how handsome Royden was and how easily so many beauties fell into his arms, he could understand why he had no wish to be hurried up the aisle with a young girl.

In a short time he might find that she had nothing new to offer him and would become dull and dreary in his eyes.

However, it was not the sort of comment he could make to his friend.

So he merely replied,

"I am very sorry to hear that you are not as strong as you would like to be, Edward, but take life easy and you will doubtless live to be a centenarian."

"I am serious, Arthur, in what I am about to say," the Earl said sharply. "Therefore I want you to use your brain to help me, as I would help you if you needed it in any emergency."

"Of course I will help you, Edward, if that is what you want, but I doubt if Royden will listen to me any more than he will listen to you. He is enjoying life and who can blame him? It is what we would certainly have done at his age and you and I cannot deny that that is the truth!"

Even as he spoke, he felt that he was being slightly tactless.

His friend's wife, who, in his opinion, had been a somewhat dull woman, had died four years ago.

She had considerably disappointed her husband in that she was only able to give him one child and that was Royden.

It was rather strange that the two men, who were close neighbours, as their estates bordered each other, had both suffered in the same way over their marriages.

The Earl had married a girl who had seemed, at the time, an exceedingly good choice.

After they were married and had produced the one precious son, she had found it impossible to have another child. She had gone from doctor to doctor, but they could only tell her that there was nothing they could do to help her.

Because he was so close a friend of the Earl's and they were neighbours in the country, he knew, as no one else knew, how much the Earl suffered at the thought of his illustrious family, who had played such an important part in the history of England for the last three centuries, losing their immense influence through lack of an heir.

For the past ten years the present Earl had always been in attendance on the Queen at Windsor Castle.

And only when he had retired to the country did he begin to worry about his son's marriage.

He had become almost obsessed by the idea that Royden must marry and have a large number of children in case the name died out and the huge ancestral home was empty.

Lord Waverstone drank a little more of his coffee before he observed,

"I cannot believe, Edward, that you have come up from the country especially to tell me what I know already. What other news have you to surprise me with?"

"I have thought it over for some time and I have come to the conclusion, Arthur, that there is only one way to make Royden see any sense. And that is to force him, however unpleasant it may be for him, into marriage."

Lord Waverstone sighed.

He had heard this before and he was quite certain that Royden would fight every inch of the way to remain single and unattached.

"I have therefore decided," the Earl said, speaking slowly and distinctly, "that the only possibility of making Royden see sense is to make him marry your daughter."

Lord Waverstone jumped and for a brief moment his coffee was in danger of being spilt.

As he put it down, he exclaimed,

"Marry Malva! My dear Edward, I am sure it's the last thing Royden would ever want to do and I am almost certain that Malva would feel the same about him."

He hesitated for a moment before he added,

"After all she is only twenty. Because my wife was ill for so long she has not really been a *debutante* in the full meaning of the word. And she has only come to London occasionally instead of having a Season here as she should do."

"But now poor Edith is dead," the Earl said, "Malva will undoubtedly come to London and a great number of young men will find her charming and beautiful. Then, as far as I am concerned, she will be lost to both me and my son."

It suddenly struck Lord Waverstone for the first time that it would be, as far as he was concerned, a perfect marriage if Malva would agree to it.

The two estates would join each other and the estate that had been in the Earl's family for so many generations was treble the size of Lord Waverstone's.

Also Hillingwood Towers, which had been in the possession of the family since the reign of Queen Elizabeth was not only magnificent but contained some of the most famous pictures to be seen anywhere in the country.

He could imagine that most girls would jump at the opportunity of being married to Royden however difficult he might be at times.

But Malva was different from other young women.

She had already said to her father that she had no intention of getting married quickly as most of her friends were anxious to do.

She was perfectly content to be at home with him, especially when she could ride his horses and that would please her far more than dancing at endless London parties or trotting up and down Rotten Row in some fashionable and expensive outfit.

Because he so enjoyed the company of his daughter when he was at home and, because she had been so very attentive to her mother until she died, Lord Waverstone had not concerned himself greatly with the thought of his daughter marrying or if she would make a good choice when it came to the point.

Now he could not help thinking that nothing could be so satisfactory as Royden marrying Malva.

They could then join the two estates together and they would be the most envied couple in the whole of the Social world.

Although Lord Waverstone was well off and had no reason to worry, he was not in the same field as his friend, the Earl of Hillingwood.

He was undoubtedly one of the richest men in the country and his horses, which won so many classic races, were superb.

Yet he had in fact never thought for one moment that his friend's son, who was the most sought after and eligible young man in the whole of London, should marry his daughter.

It was not only the difference in their ages that had blinded him to the fact of how suitable such a marriage could be.

It was also because he had always thought of Malva as a child and he had not really ever considered her to be of marriageable age.

Yet she would be twenty-one in two months' time.

It struck him as it had never done before that he should by now have had her presented at Court.

And she should certainly take her place among the *debutantes* who attended all the parties in the Season and made sure they received a great deal of attention whenever they appeared in public.

Because of his wife's protracted illness and now her death, Lord Waverstone had been in the country since Malva had left school.

She had seemed totally happy riding her father's horses and attending to her mother who she adored.

When he had left home this morning in answer to the letter from his friend asking to meet him at White's Club, he had never for one moment thought that this was the reason why the Earl wanted to see him so urgently.

Yet now he could not help feeling again that it was a proposition that could well be of considerable advantage to his daughter and to him.

"Well, Edward, what do you want me to do?" he now asked.

"I want you to talk to Malva in the same way I will talk to Royden and we will make it clear to both of them that this is their destiny and we do *not* wish to argue about it."

Lord Waverstone could not help thinking that while he was uncertain of Malva's attitude he was quite sure that Royden, who only liked older women and those who were married, would take up a very different one.

There was no doubt that he was talked about by every gossip in London.

But they had to admit that while he was attracted to the most beautiful women in the *Beau Monde* his *affaires-de-coeur* never lasted long.

In fact by the time the husband in question began to get angry and talked about having a duel, young Royden had already moved on to someone else and was no longer a menace.

Aloud Lord Waverstone remarked,

"I can understand, Edward, that you are anxious for Royden to have a family. Equally you would not wish him to be unhappy or worse still to have a divorce."

The Earl held up his hands in horror.

"There has never been a divorce in my family since we first became of note in the reign of King Canute. And I will make certain that it does not happen in this century at any rate!"

"So what do you want me to do?" Lord Waverstone asked again.

"I want you to talk to your daughter and, as we have a house party coming to the races that I have arranged for next week, you must bring her, looking charming as she always does. I am sure that after I have spoken to Royden that there will be no more difficulties."

Lord Waverstone thought that there might easily be a great many of them.

First of all Royden would refuse to marry Malva or any other girl who was, in his opinion, too young and inexperienced to be of any interest to him.

But he knew that it was no use whatever saying so to the Earl, who was determined to have his own way as usual.

It was obvious that once and for all he wanted to provide his family with the heir it needed to carry on his illustrious lineage.

Aloud Lord Waverstone said,

"Of course I will do, Edward. At the same time I think you should be tactful about this proposed marriage. It's not going to be easy for Royden, who is having such a good time, to settle down. I cannot help thinking that he has no idea that Malva is as old as she is and in point of fact now grown up and a young lady."

"We have to make both my son and your daughter do as they are told," the Earl insisted. "I will speak to Royden before we go down to the country and make it very clear to him that he is to do his duty and that is to marry and have children."

One again Lord Waverstone was thinking that there were a great many problems about this proposition from his old friend and neighbour.

But he thought it was no use him arguing in support of Royden, but leave him to do his own fighting, which he was sure he was capable of doing.

"I will certainly do what I can, Edward," he said, "But I have a feeling that it will be more difficult than you think. You must therefore use a great deal of patience and it would be a great mistake for either of us to start fighting with our children."

As he spoke, he saw the Earl's lips tighten and he knew that, because he was so determined to have his own way, he was quite prepared to fight for it if it became at all necessary.

"Now, Edward, I must be getting back to the House of Lords," he said. "There is a very important motion this afternoon which I have to discuss with Her Majesty the Queen and there are certain people I have to see before it actually takes place."

"I quite understand," the Earl replied. "But I will expect you at The Towers on Thursday night for dinner at our usual time of eight o'clock."

He paused before he added,

"Actually, now I think about it, it would be a good idea for you to stay the night."

Lord Waverstone turned to look at him in surprise.

"But we are less than a mile away," he pointed out.

"Yes, but there is always the endless fuss of having a carriage waiting and you cannot keep the horses up too long. No, you stay with me, Arthur. It will be easier then for the two young people to get to know each other better than they do at present."

"It seems extraordinary as we live so near that they don't know each other better," Lord Waterstone said. "At the same time you must be patient, Edward, and realise that the marriage of my daughter is a very serious matter and she may not wish to leave me so soon after her mother's unfortunate death."

"I can well understand that," the Earl replied. "But, as she is very pretty, it would be a great mistake for her to be snatched up by another man who would not be able to offer her anything as prestigious as Royden can."

Lord Waverstone knew that this was the truth and so he thought it a mistake to argue over the matter.

"We will naturally be delighted to be your guests, Edward," he replied.

"As it is so important for Malva to look her best," the Earl said, "I think you should persuade her not to wear black but white. As she is so young it is permissible in the circumstances and will not have the depressing effect that a black dress of mourning always has on a young woman at a ball."

"That is very sensible of you," Lord Waverstone said. "I am sure that, as we are in the country, she need not at any time appear in mourning, although I am sure that she will not wish to wear very bright colours."

He only hoped that his daughter had the right sort of clothes that were not black to wear at the Earl's house party.

There was no point in discussing it with the Earl as he invariably expected his orders to be obeyed at once. And he therefore became irritated if crossed in any way.

'I am sure that Malva will be all right one way or another,' he thought, as he rose to his feet and said,

"Goodbye Edward. We will come to you, if it is all right, on Wednesday night. And, if your party is arriving on Thursday, it would be a good idea for the young people to get to know each other before there is any question of any of your guests having an idea of what you are now planning."

"*We* are planning," the Earl countered firmly. "It is absolutely essential that we don't waste any time but marry them off as soon as we possibly can."

It did pass through Lord Waverstone's mind that such haste would appear most unfeeling when his wife had only been dead for six months.

Queen Victoria had made rules for mourning to be extended to as long as a year and from Her Majesty's point of view it would be totally impossible for the daughter of a deceased woman not to wear black and nothing but black for at least twelve months.

But, as he told himself, this was surely exceptional circumstances and the Earl had to bring off this marriage before any more time was wasted in case he was no longer there to direct events with his usual rod of iron.

Lord Waverstone rose to his feet.

"I will look forward to seeing you on Wednesday, Edward. I can only hope that everything will go as you want it to, but young people have minds of their own, you know."

"Then they should be taught to do as they are told," the Earl said sharply. "That is absolutely vital as far as my son is concerned."

Lord Waverstone did not then volunteer an opinion about his daughter Malva's reaction to the idea and it was something he had not thought about before.

Of course as she had been brought up in the shadow of The Towers, so to speak, it was very obvious that she was extremely impressed by the beauty of the house and all its precious treasures.

Also he knew that the one thing that attracted her to it more than anything else were the horses.

Although he himself had spent quite a considerable amount of money on buying the best horseflesh available, he knew that he could not compete in any way with those that belonged to his friend, the Earl.

'But I can hardly ask my daughter to marry a man because he has good horses,' he told himself, 'but, as every woman seems to fall head over heels in love with Royden immediately, there is no reason why Malva should not do the same.'

The idea cheered him up as he later drove towards Windsor Castle.

He had in fact found it rather difficult to listen to the motion in the House of Lords the Queen wanted him to report to her on, for the simple reason he kept thinking of what the Earl had said to him at White's.

However, he could only tell himself that no woman, old or young, could help being impressed by The Towers and all women found Royden an irresistible lover.

At the same time before he reached Windsor Castle he was feeling that, whatever happened in the near future, it was not going to be as his friend, the Earl, anticipated.

*

The Earl, driving back from White's to his house in Park Lane was thinking over what he would say to his son.

How he must be absolutely firm in his decision that he was to stop playing around and settle down as a married man.

'He can take over The Towers,' the Earl thought, 'and I will go North to Scotland to my house there which I have always found most comfortable. The grouse shooting and fishing are certainly better than anything we have in the South.'

He was so busy working things out as he wanted them to be that it was with a start he realised that he was outside his house in Park Lane.

As the Earl now stepped out of his carriage, a horse drew up ridden by his son, who had just returned at that moment from Rotten Row.

The two of them walked up the steps together and in through the front door.

"I want to speak to you, Royden," the Earl said as soon as they were inside, "so come now into the study."

"I am in rather a hurry, Papa," he replied. "I have a luncheon engagement and I must change my clothes. You know how angry a hostess can become if her guests arrive late."

"I have the idea, Royden, that your luncheon party consists of just two people. You must therefore excuse me if I take up a little of your time."

Royden laughed.

"You always hit the nail on the head, Papa, and you have done so again. She is very pretty and has a wit which most English women lack. In case you are curious, I will tell you that she is French and only arrived in London from Paris two days ago. But I am seeing her for dinner and she will not be at the luncheon party."

By the time he had finished speaking, Royden was half way up the stairs and the Earl knew that it would be impossible to stop him.

"Very well," he now said, "if you must keep your engagements, I will not prevent you from doing so. But I wish to speak to you as soon as you can tear yourself away and come back here. It is very important!"

"I will do my best," Royden shouted, as he reached the landing. "But I make no false promises, Papa."

He had disappeared into his room before the Earl could reply.

A little later he heard his voice in the hall and knew he was setting off again to meet some pretty Frenchwoman who certainly was a newcomer to his tally of beauties.

*

It was in fact not until the following day that the Earl had his serious talk with his son.

During which time the whole scenario had been going over and over in his mind.

Finally on the Monday as they were to leave on the Wednesday for the country for the party which was to be at The Towers before the race meeting, Royden joined his father in his study in the middle of the afternoon.

"I am home early," he said, "because the luncheon party I went to was spoilt by having too many people. The majority of them being conversational bores, who talked on and on without pausing and at the end of it all had said nothing but a lot of hot air."

The Earl laughed.

"I know exactly what you mean, Royden. But what I have to say to you is very different and a matter I have been trying to bring to your attention for several days."

"I do know, Papa, and you must forgive me, but I never seem to have a moment to myself when I am in London. In point of fact at almost every party I go to there are hostesses reproaching me because I have not been to theirs or left almost before I arrived."

He threw himself down in one of the easy chairs as he spoke.

The Earl had to admit that he was an extremely good-looking young man.

Because he was so active he was thin and perfectly proportioned.

He was over six feet tall and his square shoulders seemed to accentuate his exceedingly handsome face.

It was not surprising, the Earl thought to himself, that so many women fell in love with him. He had only to look in their direction and they were ready to run into his arms.

"Now what is it, Papa?" Royden asked. "And if I have offended you in any way, then I am more than ready to apologise before you say anything more."

"You have not offended me," his father replied. "I only want you to think seriously about your future."

He was aware as he spoke that his son stiffened as if he sensed what was coming.

The Earl went on somewhat quickly,

"As you will doubtless remember, I have spoken to you before about you getting married, but it is essential that you should do so now. Therefore I have chosen your wife for you."

"*Chosen a wife for me!*" Royden exclaimed. "But that is most unfair, Papa. After all I have to marry her, not you!"

"Just let me explain to you what I have planned," the Earl carried on, ignoring his son's hostile reaction.

Because he anticipated what was coming, there was a wary look in Royden's eyes as he sat up a little more in the chair.

"When we have talked about you getting married," his father said, "you have told me that you are in no hurry. In the past that seemed reasonable enough. But now the doctors have told me that there is some slight damage to my heart which may shorten my life considerably."

"I am very sorry to hear that, Papa."

"I don't want your sympathy," the Earl snapped. "But, when it happens, I only hope that it's quick and that I don't linger on as so many people do."

"I feel sure you are exaggerating, Papa," Royden replied. "No one could ride as you do and not be in good health."

The Earl thought that his son was very quick with his answers.

Therefore he said,

"What I want to discuss with you is the future. If I am too ill to carry on doing what I am doing at present then I am thinking of moving to the North and leaving you in charge of The Towers."

His son did not reply and he went on rapidly,

"You know, as well as I do, that you cannot live there alone. It is absolutely essential that you should have a wife to help you."

He paused for a moment before he continued,

"Not just with the house itself but with the horses, the Racecourse and the garden that has grown considerably in the last few years and is the envy of every gardener in the country."

"I am well aware of all that," Royden managed to say. "But I have no wish to marry anyone I know at this moment and, as you yourself will agree, being married is a serious matter and the last thing you would want, I am sure, Papa, is a divorce in the family."

"A divorce!" the Earl expostulated. "It is something we must never have. It would be an utter disgrace to us all."

"I agree, Papa," Royden replied, "that is why I have no intention of marrying in a hurry."

"As I have no idea how long I will live," the Earl said, "I want to leave everything in the very best order possible."

There was silence.

Then the Earl said slowly,

"I have therefore chosen a wife for you, who I think will be a great asset to the family and with whom there is no reason for you to be unhappy."

For a moment Royden was stunned into silence.

Then, as he opened his lips to protest at the whole idea, the Earl said,

"The person I have chosen for you is Malva Stone, the daughter of our nearest neighbour, who will, I believe, grace the position you offer her. It will make both me and her father exceedingly happy and satisfied by the union."

Royden jumped up from the chair and walked to the window.

As he gazed out at the fine array of flowers in the garden, he said,

"I just cannot imagine, Papa, anything more horrific than being tied to a woman one does not love and be forced to spend the rest of one's life with her."

"If she gives you children and if she performs her duty as a wife, I cannot see any reason why you should complain."

"But Papa, I have no wish to be married to anyone, least of all to a girl who I hardly know and who I have not seen since she was in a pram."

"Lord Waverstone is my oldest friend," his father interrupted. "His daughter is acclaimed as very beautiful and is charming, as her mother was. It is a tragedy that Lady Waverstone is dead and I think that we owe it to his Lordship to help him in every way we can."

He stopped for breath before he went on,

"Nothing could be better than for us to join his land with ours and for his daughter and you to make it a really glorious and magnificent home for your children."

"But I have already told you, Papa," Royden said, his voice rising, "that I will not marry anyone until I find it impossible to live without her."

As he spoke, the Earl sat down in his chair and put one hand to his heart and the other pressed over his eyes.

"You are – upsetting me," he murmured in a voice which indicated that every word was difficult to say. "You are upsetting me a great deal and I cannot – listen to you at the moment – "

His words were difficult to hear and his Lordship looked as if he would slump forward onto the writing table.

Royden reached for the bell and rang it jerkily.

It was only a few moments before the door opened and a footman came in.

"His Lordship is not feeling well," Royden called out sharply. "Send immediately for his doctor and tell his valet to help him upstairs."

The footman ran off to obey his orders.

Then the Earl took his hand from his eyes and said,

"I don't want a doctor. What I want, my son, is for you to obey me and make me a happy man before I die."

Royden did not answer.

He walked to the window, knowing that his father was acting the part, but it was impossible for him to say so.

Only when the Earl's valet had brought him a phial of his medicine, followed by a glass of champagne to take away the nasty taste, did he turn from the window to say,

"I will think over what you have said, Papa, but I know when you have made up your mind about anything, as you have at the moment, it is impossible to argue with you."

The Earl did not answer.

But, as Royden turned towards the window again, there was a faint smile on his lips.

CHAPTER TWO

After Lord Waverstone had left Windsor Castle, he went to Number 10 Downing Street as the Prime Minister had sent for him.

After he had settled a number of different questions that had been printed in the newspapers and were decidedly controversial in the country, he was driven on to his house in the heart of Chelsea.

It was a very attractive house, but not a large one and he and his wife had furnished it with exquisite taste when they had first married.

Every room seemed to speak to him of her.

As he entered the house, he told the butler to inform his daughter that he had returned home.

So he was not surprised when a few minutes later the door was flung open and Malva came running in.

"Papa, you are back early!" she exclaimed. "I did not expect you until later, but it is lovely to see you. Now for once I can have you to myself."

Lord Waverstone smiled and replied,

"That is exactly what I want as I have so much to tell you and to talk to you about."

Malva sat down on the sofa and asked,

"What has happened now, Papa?"

"Nothing frightening, but certainly unusual," Lord Waverstone replied. "I want you to listen very attentively to what I am going to tell you."

"I always do," she replied. "As you know, Papa, I see far too little of you and I am counting the days until we can go back to the country and ride our wonderful horses again."

"So am I," her father answered. "But there is a proposition which I have to put in front of you. I want you to consider it very carefully and not make up your mind until you have thought it out in every detail."

"You are making me curious. What can it be?"

"That is exactly what I am going to tell you," Lord Waverstone said. "As I told you before I left this morning, I had a very special message from the Earl of Hillingwood, asking me to meet him at White's."

"I remember that, Papa, and I wondered why he wanted to see you."

"He wanted to see me," he said slowly, "because his one desire in life is that you should marry his son!"

Malva stared at her father as if she thought that he must be playing games with her.

Then, as she saw by the expression on his face that he was serious, she breathed,

"Did the Earl really say that? Are you quite certain it was not a joke?"

"No, it was no joke. He made it very clear that the one thing he wants is that we should unite our estates into one and, of course, you and Royden will run it from The Towers."

While he was speaking rather slowly and distinctly, his daughter was staring at him incredulously.

Then she said,

"He must be pulling your leg, Papa. You know as well as I do that everyone in London is aware that Royden is determined not to marry and spends his entire time with beautiful ladies who are already married and so they cannot take him up the aisle."

She spoke the words sharply and her father retorted,

"Yes, I know that, my dearest Malva, but the Earl is terrified that his son will not marry at all and when he himself dies it will be the end of the very long history of his family."

There was silence for a moment.

Then Lord Waverstone continued,

"Because he is so terrified that might happen, he is determined that his son shall be married. It's quite obvious that you are a suitable wife for him in every possible way. Of course if our lands were joined it will make The Towers even more impressive than it is already."

"What you are telling me takes my breath away," Malva murmured. "What does Royden say to this idea?"

"That, of course, I was not told, but, as the Earl has set his heart upon it and is determined with every means in his power to see that the marriage takes place, I can only suppose that Royden will give in to his father."

"And I think he will not," Malva asserted. "As he lives next door and, as you know, people talk about him all the time, I have been informed of almost every *affaire-de-coeur* he has had these past two or three years and they certainly do *not* include anyone of my age."

"Or anyone who he could marry," Lord Waverstone replied.

"Well, for one thing I have no wish to marry him or anyone else at the moment," Malva declared. "I love being with you, Papa, and I am very happy as I am."

There was silence.

And then Lord Waverstone said,

"You make it very difficult for me not to consider what the Earl has suggested. After all, as you well know, he is a very old friend of mine."

"What do you want me to consider, Papa?" Malva asked. "I want to marry someone I love and I know Mama wanted me to do that. She often told me how you and she had fallen in love with each other from the moment you first met."

Lord Waverstone made a strange sound, but he did not speak.

And Malva went on,

"Mama told me it was the most wonderful moment of her life when she looked into your eyes and knew that you were feeling exactly the same way as she did. Look how happy you were. I never knew that people could be so blissfully happy or so much in love until I watched you and Mama together."

"I know, I know," Lord Waverstone muttered, as if it was agony to hear what his daughter was saying.

Then he seemed to shake himself and stated firmly,

"At the same time we have to face facts. As I will not live for ever, you will have to marry someone sooner or later and who could be more suitable than the Viscount Royden with The Towers and our land joined together?"

He paused for a moment and then continued,

"And you would make a very beautiful Countess of Hillingwood, my dearest Malva."

"I would make a very unhappy one until I left the man I had been forced to marry," Malva replied stoutly.

There was silence.

It was a long silence because her father sat waiting, thinking that it would be wrong to press her too strongly at this stage.

"I think you have forgotten one thing," Malva said unexpectedly. "I am in mourning for at least another four months. You know as well as I do that Her Majesty frowns on anyone who comes out of black in what in her opinion is too soon."

She spread out her hands as she added,

"I hate black. It's depressing and unbecoming, but what else can I do?"

"Nothing, my dearest. The one thing it would be impossible for either of us to do would be to offend Her Majesty. She has always treated me with great kindness and I can assure you that it is very flattering for me that she consults me so often on matters which she believes I am more knowledgeable about than my contemporaries."

"Of course you are, Papa, and I think, if you are honest you will realise that Her Majesty really likes tall handsome men around her and you are certainly that."

Lord Waverstone laughed.

Then he said,

"If I don't wish to offend Her Majesty, I certainly don't want to offend the Earl. As we live next door to each other and share so many interests, including our horses, it would be a disaster if he became angry with us and we were not on speaking terms."

"Then what can we do?" Malva asked despairingly. "I have no wish to marry his son or anyone else for that matter."

There was silence for quite some minutes.

Then Lord Waverstone said,

"What I suggest, my dearest, is that you don't say immediately that marrying Viscount Royden is something you would never do. I think that the way to handle this very difficult matter is for you to talk to him. I expect you will find that he is just as anxious to remain single as you are. In fact when it comes to fighting against the marriage I think that you will be able to leave it to him."

"I did not think of that, Papa," she answered him. "You are very astute to do so."

"What I am thinking," Lord Waverstone continued, "is that we will go to the country and, while we are there on our own ground, so to speak, you meet Royden and tell him your feelings quite frankly, which I am almost certain will be the same as his. Then leave him to get us out of the difficulties as pleasantly and as expeditiously as possible."

Malva clapped her hands.

"You are so clever, Papa. I might have guessed that you would find a solution to this nonsense. After all, if you can do it for the Queen, you can certainly do it for me!"

Lord Waverstone chuckled.

"I certainly hope I am right, but I am quite certain if Royden is immersed in love affairs with older and married women, he will have no desire to be married to a young girl. Even if we combine all our horses that will not be enough temptation!"

He was speaking slowly and his daughter laughed.

"Of course you are right, Papa, you are always right about things like that. As you so rightly say, it would be a great mistake to quarrel with the Earl. After all I am allowed to ride all his horses when I wish to do so and ever since I could read I have been permitted to borrow books from his fabulous library and I sincerely think that I would miss his books more than anything else if we were to be at daggers drawn."

"That is something that we must not be under any circumstances," Lord Waverstone said. "If you have your perks from The Towers, so do I. Not only have his horses been at my disposal but his carriages as well. And it would embarrass me to think how often I drive in his quicker and far more up to date carriages to Windsor Castle than I do in my own."

"Of course you do, Papa. Otherwise they would stand in the stables month after month without being used."

"I should be most uncomfortable if I did not use them," Lord Waverstone confessed. "There are also a good number of other small things that we share because we are neighbours which would make it not only difficult for me to do without them but I would find it very expensive."

"I know exactly what you mean, Papa. Therefore I agree we must be careful not to offend the Earl. At the same time I *cannot* and will not marry his son."

"But you must not say so, my dearest, except, of course, to young Royden. I think it is what he will want to hear anyway."

Malva gave a deep sigh.

"Very well, Papa, you arrange for us to meet, but make it very clear that we have a great deal of talking to do before any final decision is reached."

"One thing is quite certain," her father said, "I don't want to lose you. Equally I have told myself many times I must not be greedy. If you do fall in love, my dearest, I will try not to think that I have lost a daughter, but gained a son."

Malva, who was standing near him, bent down and kissed him.

"You are always very sensible, Papa. I am sure that is why the Queen likes you so much. So many people are hysterical about themselves and, of course, are always very certain that their way is the best."

"That is the sort of flattery I like," he replied. "But we must be very careful, as I have already told you, not to upset his Lordship. If he is very angry, let his son bear the brunt of his anger."

"I will certainly do so, Papa, and I might even point out to him that there are plenty of other young women of far greater consequence than I am who would jump at the idea of being his wife simply because they would then be the Mistress of Hillingwood Towers."

Lord Waverstone opened his lips as if he was about to say something and then changed his mind and remained silent.

He was actually thinking that it would make him very happy if his daughter was the Mistress of The Towers, but it would be wrong for him to say so and upset Malva.

He could only hope that perhaps by some miracle she and Royden would find that they had a closer affinity than they had at the moment.

Perhaps, although it might take quite a long time, they could develop a real affection for each other.

Then he told himself that he was only dreaming.

Royden, although still a young man, was too old to change his ways and certainly not to marry a girl who was so much younger than he was.

Even though he was quite certain that he would have to go a long way before he found anyone as attractive or intelligent as Malva.

'But I am prejudiced,' he told himself.

Then he began to open the letters waiting for him on his table.

*

It was the day after they arrived in the country that Malva was riding one of the fastest of her father's horses when she realised that there was a man coming out of the wood that bordered their estate with the Earl's.

One glance told her instantly who it was.

She deliberately turned her horse round and started to ride in the opposite direction.

She had lain awake for several nights thinking over what her father had said to her, and how she had been very positive that she would not marry Royden even though she realised how exceedingly tactful she had to be in refusing him.

'How shall I do it? How exactly shall I do it?' she asked herself a dozen times.

Now, at the sight of Royden, she realised that she had not yet come to any conclusion.

She was therefore determined to move out of sight as quickly as possible.

After she had turned her horse away in the opposite direction from him, she suddenly thought that it would be far too obvious if she immediately broke into a gallop.

So she started to ride quicker but without obviously running away.

'I cannot see him just yet,' she told herself. 'I must think out exactly what I will say to him before we meet."

Because, when he came down to the country, it was usually at weekends, she had not expected Royden to be here so soon.

Yet, she reflected, perhaps like her, he had thought that he must run away from London and felt that his brain would be sharper and more intelligent in the clean warm air of the countryside.

She had almost reached the edge of the field when she heard the hammer of hooves close behind her and then guessed that Royden must have spotted her.

He had therefore crossed the fields quicker than she expected.

In fact, even as she turned her head, she found him beside her.

He was riding a horse that she knew was one of the fastest and best jumpers in the whole of the Earl's stables.

"Good morning, Malva," Royden called out, lifting his hat.

Because she thought it tactful, Malva managed to look at him with an expression of surprise.

"I had no idea you were at The Towers," she said. "I thought that you were in London enjoying the delights of the Season. In fact all the newspapers have mentioned it."

Royden laughed.

Although she had no wish to say it, Malva had to admit that he was very handsome.

"The newspapers are just a menace," he replied. "I have come to the country because I understood from my father you are fully aware that he has presented us with a very difficult problem."

"I am glad you admit it is difficult," Malva replied. "I cannot help but feel that it's a strange way of receiving a proposal of marriage."

She thought as she spoke that it was better to go straight to the point under the circumstances.

And to make it clear from the very beginning that she was not impressed or particularly flattered by the Earl wanting her as his daughter-in-law.

"What I suggest we do," Royden said, "is to ride to the lake and sit in comfort in the Pavilion while we discuss what is a very serious matter for both of us."

He spoke in what she thought was a very pleasant way and it would appear rude and unfeeling if she refused.

"Very well," she agreed. "Give me a fair start and I will race you to the lake. I know you are riding one of the fastest horses in your stables, but I am also proud of the speed that Mayflower can achieve if he wants to."

"I will now count to ten," Royden said. "You must admit that is a fair start."

"It depends how fast you count," Malva argued. "I can only request that you do it as slowly and as clearly as if you were on a Racecourse."

"I will try," he promised.

Mayflower was only too glad to stretch his legs and Malva knew that he could be very fast on the flat.

There was a clear piece of land in front of them that stretched towards The Towers.

The lake, which was an artificial one put in by one of the previous Earls, was just beyond the point where the two estates joined each other.

Malva was travelling so fast that she thought at first she would have an easy victory.

Then, as she heard Royden's horse, she knew that it was going to be more of a contest than she had anticipated.

She pushed Mayflower and, as she did so, she was quite certain that Royden really wanted to win the race.

He had always wanted to win everything he took part in ever since he had been a small child.

When she had first known him and he was at school she had thought that he was determined to be a winner at every game that took his fancy.

In fact she had often thought that he was conceited and too proud of himself to be considered by her seriously even though he had lived next door.

He had gone through the usual phase of believing that girls were inferior and a nuisance.

At one time, when she was about ten years old and he was eight years older, she had disliked him thoroughly and thought him to be unnecessarily pleased with himself.

But, as the years passed and they encountered each other more frequently if only casually, she had to admit that he had excellent manners.

If he was talking to someone, he managed to make that person feel he was really interested in them as well as what they were saying.

There was no doubt that they were very fond of him on the Hillingwood estate and the workers spoke warmly of the young Master.

"He be a good un," one man had said to Malva. "We be proud to work for 'im and to please 'im."

That, Malva knew, was high praise from those who lived on the estate and by the estate and it was very much the same as they always said about her father.

Now, when she had just about reached the edge of the lake a few lengths ahead of him, he swept past her.

To her annoyance he was obviously there first.

"I have won! I have won!" he crowed as she joined him. "That, as you know, Malva, is what I have tried to do ever since we were children."

"It is what you have always done," she responded. "And it's very bad for you. But on this occasion I have to admit, although it hurts me to do so, that Solomon is faster than Mayflower."

"All the same I am a great admirer of Mayflower," he commented. "I hope you will let me ride him one day to see if I can get him to exert himself a little more than you can."

"Now you are insulting me as a rider," Malva said, "which I greatly resent."

"I have certainly never insulted you. In fact I think you are the best woman rider I have ever seen, Malva, and that is not flattery but the truth."

They tied the horses up on a post by the lake.

Then they walked towards the Pavilion where there were comfortable seats facing the water.

Malva sat in one of them and Royden sat beside her.

"I suppose you know what I want to talk to you about," he began.

Malva nodded.

"My father told me after he had seen your father. To be truthful I was totally astonished and horrified at the idea."

"Why horrified?" he asked.

"Because I have no wish to marry anyone unless I love him and he loves me with all his heart and soul, which is very difficult to find at any time."

She spoke very quietly.

Royden looked surprised before he said,

"I somehow thought from what my father said that you would be delighted at the idea.

"Were *you* delighted?" Malva asked him.

For a moment Royden hesitated.

Then, as if he could not help himself, he blurted out,

"To be honest I was appalled and shocked. I think I should be truthful and say right away that I have no wish to marry anyone."

"That is what I heard about you," Malva replied. "I do sympathise because I feel exactly the same."

"You do surprise me, Malva, I was expecting you to be thrilled and charmed at the idea of reigning at The Towers in glory."

There was complete silence for a while as Malva tried to think how of she could possibly express what she was feeling without, in any way, being rude.

Then, as if he sensed what was going through her mind, he said,

"If you really have no wish to marry me, would it not be best to say so frankly?"

"I was hoping that you would take the initiative," Malva countered rather bravely.

For a moment Royden stared at her.

Then he laughed.

"Very well, if you want to be honest and I think that we should be with each other, I have no wish to marry anyone."

"But your father insists that you should, Royden."

"I know and he has told me that it will break his heart and doubtless take him to an early grave if I don't produce an heir, which I do agree is essential at some point in the future for the sake of my family."

"Then it should not be very difficult for you to find any number of very suitable women who would be only too thrilled to be your wife," Malva suggested.

"I know that, but I should always be thinking that they had married Hillingwood Towers rather than me and quite frankly anyway I want to be free," Royden replied.

"I suppose quite a number of men feel like that, but at least you are frank about it."

"Surprisingly you are not offended at my being so," he smiled. "I think you are like your father who is known to settle every problem which is brought to him with a tact that makes him one of the most favoured advisers to Her Majesty at Windsor Castle."

"I have heard that," Malva replied, "and I am sure it is true. Papa finds an answer to everyone's problems, but I have a feeling that he does not wish to find an answer to this one."

"Why?" Royden asked abruptly.

"Because he wants to see me as the Queen of The Towers," Malva answered.

"For that, of course, I have to be the King," Royden parried sarcastically.

"There is no one else as you well know," Malva replied. "If you had a brother or a number of brothers, it would have made things very much easier."

"I know that," he answered. "I expect you know, as everyone else does, that after I was born my mother was told that she could not have another child and it almost broke my father's heart."

"I think he was very lucky to have you. You can, of course, make it up to him very easily for what he has missed."

"Not at all easily," Royden said sharply. "As I have told you and we agreed to being frank, I have no wish to marry you or indeed anyone else. I want to be free, I want to travel over the world as I have done recently and I want to enjoy myself in my own way without being tied down."

He spoke almost angrily.

Then Malva said softly,

"I can understand why you feel like that and I am very sorry for you. But I do think that you must help your father and surely there must be one person in the world you could find happiness with if she becomes your wife."

"I cannot think of one single person – "

"Then what can we do?" Malva asked.

To her surprise Royden then rose from the seat and walked down to the water's edge.

He stared hard at the lake as if he was asking it the burning question.

Malva thought it would be a mistake to interrupt him, so she sat still waiting for him to come back.

After several minutes he turned round and walked back to her.

"When I was thinking this over last night," he said, "I had an idea which I was sure came to me in answer to my request for help."

Malva smiled.

"I think you mean it came from the stars. I have often done that. I have looked up at the stars and prayed for them to tell me the answer to my question."

"Then have you asked them to answer this one?" he enquired.

"I did not think about it until this moment," Malva replied. "But it is something I might easily do tonight."

"While I thought I had an answer, it seems too fantastic and I had no intention of telling you about it, but now if you are absolutely determined, as you have just said, not to marry me, I will tell you my idea."

"I can tell you honestly, cross my heart," Malva repeated, "that I have no wish to marry anyone unless I was in love with him and he was really in love with me."

"I respect you for that," he answered. "So listen to this idea, although you may think it absolute nonsense."

"I will listen to any idea that will in some way leave your father and mine happy with their ambitions for you and me, but leave us with our freedom."

"That is exactly what I want," Royden agreed. "If we can pull this off, we can manage to do that and I am sure you will agree with me that it is the only possible way we can remain free."

Malva sat back further in her chair.

"I am listening," she breathed.

He sat down in the chair he had sat in before.

"Now, as you must realise," he started, "my father is completely determined that I will get married. In fact he made it very clear to me when he told me what he wanted that if I did not agree I might easily be causing his death."

Malva made an exclamation of horror, but she did not interrupt and Royden continued,

"What we might do therefore, if you agree, is to *pretend* that we were married."

Malva stared at him.

"How on earth can we do that?" she asked.

"Well, I think that the one card we do actually hold in our hands is the fact that you are still in mourning for at least another four months."

Malva nodded to agree that this was true, but did not say anything.

"Now what I suggest we do," Royden said, "is to let our two fathers start planning a large wedding which I should dislike intensely, which we can, however, point out is extremely wrong from your father's point of view and might incur the condemnation of the Queen."

"I am sure that's the truth," Malva answered. "Her Majesty is still in mourning for her Prince Albert and she cannot understand why everyone does not wish to drape themselves in gloomy black in the same way that she does all the time."

"It's an obsession with her," Royden pointed out. "But it could be useful to us."

"Tell me exactly how," Malva quizzed him.

"Well, we go to our fathers and say that, as we are horrified at the idea of a grand wedding with the bride wearing black and looking dismal, we have been married secretly either in the Chapel in Mayfair or at some private Chapel like the one we have at The Towers, where a Priest can marry two people without a Special Licence to do so."

"You mean we should pretend that is where it has taken place?" Malva asked as if she wanted to make quite certain that she was hearing his plan correctly.

"Exactly. I can easily get hold of the Certificate they give you on such an occasion, but it will not be issued by the Archbishop of Canterbury."

"What do we do then?" Malva wanted to know.

"We go back to our fathers and say we are married, but we want it kept absolutely secret until we come back from our honeymoon. Then we announce that the marriage has taken place, but we have now discovered that we are completely unsuited to each other and require a divorce."

"A divorce!" Malva exclaimed in a shocked voice.

"That is what we say we want," he replied. "I do know that our fathers will do everything in their power to prevent the Family Tree being smudged with anything so degrading as a divorce, which, as you well know, will have to go through Parliament.

Malva nodded.

Then she asked,

"What happens next?"

"It is when they are both shaken to the core and convinced that they were wrong in forcing us to marry in the first place that we admit the marriage has not actually taken place and we are completely free as we both wanted to be in the first place."

For a moment they were quiet.

Then Malva laughed.

"I never heard of anything so extraordinary and yet I have to admit *so* clever."

"I am certain," Royden said, "that, as our fathers are terrified of doing anything that will damage the family, they will be only too glad to discover that we are not in fact having to go through the Divorce Courts and will leave us time to find, in the future, the bride and bridegroom who will satisfy us as well as them."

Again they were quiet.

And then Malva sighed,

"It is certainly a very ingenious idea of yours if you really think we can carry it off."

"Of course we can, Malva. If you think it out, for one thing neither of our fathers will want anyone to know that we have been married secretly when you are still in mourning and, if you had done so, there is no doubt that Her Majesty the Queen would have been very shocked and doubtless prevented you from visiting Windsor Castle or Buckingham Palace."

"You don't think that they would expect us to wait for the next four months until it would be permissible for me at least to wear half-mourning."

"I would think from the way that my father spoke he is determined to marry us off as quickly as possible," Royden replied. "He has not really thought out the idea of you being in mourning, but, if he did, he would see that the engagement would be announced, but the marriage would not take place until September."

He smiled before he continued,

"We would have to wait, at the same time it would be impossible for us then to break off the engagement at the very last moment when the presents have poured in and doubtless a crowd of well-wishers have been invited to the Reception."

Malva put up her hands.

"It all sounds horrifying and is something I would heartily dislike anyway.

"It is something I have no intention of having, so, if we pretend we are married and they have to keep it a secret because of the Queen, where do we go?"

"Anywhere you want," he replied. "But personally I have been meaning for some time to go to the North of Africa again, which is exceedingly beautiful. At present it has very few visitors."

"That is a real adventure I would certainly enjoy," Malva replied. "But have you thought how boring it would be to have me alone for two months or if we can delay it a little, perhaps longer."

Royden smiled.

"I could put up with you for two months, but not twenty or thirty years which is the only alternative!"

"I feel the same as you," Malva said. "We can at least enjoy the voyage and it will be all very new and very exciting for me."

"The only people we will have to advise will be the seamen who serve on my yacht and who are very used to me bringing beautiful women on board. They have proved themselves not only tactful but completely loyal to me in that they have never talked to outsiders or let anyone be aware about who I was travelling with."

"Well that makes things very easy," Malva replied. "I can have a false name and, if I discard my mourning, I can be just another of your much talked about and envied *affaires-de-coeur*."

"If they are talked about, it has not been my fault," he asserted. "I am in fact very grateful that the Press have not published the names of any of the ladies in question."

"All the same I think that I should assume a false name," Malva said. "It will make it easier in the future when you take your real wife aboard if she does not learn the name of anyone she might then encounter sooner or later."

"That is indeed true," Royden agreed. "So do you really think my plan will work, Malva?"

"I see no reason why it should not do so. As you say our fathers will do everything in their power to prevent us from having a divorce so that when they finally hear and, of course, you must do it tactfully, that the Marriage Service did not take place, then they will be so relieved that we will be allowed once again to go our own ways."

"That is exactly how I worked it out. I think you are just the right person, Malva, to carry it off so that no awkward questions will be asked and we go away before anyone realises what is happening."

"Of course we must," Malva concurred.

He looked at her.

"You really mean that you will try it?"

"Well, I cannot think of any other way to avoid our fathers pushing and shoving us about and then being angry because we have not agreed to what they want," Malva replied.

"Exactly."

"Now we must work it out very cleverly," Malva continued, "as I am sure you will do. But we must make them realise it would be completely and utterly disastrous for them to tell anyone, even their close friends, that we are married. Perhaps it might be more sensible to say that we are having a trial journey together just to see if it was possible for us to wish to be married when the voyage was over."

Royden held up his hands.

"You cannot be so silly as to think that that would work," he said. "Both my father and yours would say that you had ruined your reputation because I had taken you abroad alone without a chaperone. They would say that I would have to marry you immediately to make amends for the damage I had already done."

"I did not think of that," Malva confessed. "But I suppose that they would. And I have become so used to thinking of you as a relation that it never occurred to me that to be alone with you on your yacht would be as bad Socially as cutting off my head."

"That is, of course, the reason why we have to be very careful over this and not make it obvious that, as we are not really married, they could either insist that we are married immediately or you will feel degraded for the rest of your life."

Then Malva asked him,

"Suppose when we do return and say that we want a divorce, when they find out that there is no need for one, they will insist then on us being married."

"It will be for your father to insist. But if we make it definite that we don't wish to live with each other and that you will never reign at The Towers as my wife, I think they will find that the ground has crumbled from under them. When we finally admit that the marriage is not valid and we are free after all, they will be only too pleased to agree that we can live our own separate lives in London."

Malva thought that this was somewhat unlikely.

Equally anything was better than being pushed and cajoled into marring a man she had no wish to marry and who had no wish to marry her.

"It is all rather threatening," she said, "but anything is better than you and me being tied up together and always quarrelling."

"I don't believe we would do that for a moment," Royden replied. "I have always been very fond of you and, since I have not seen you for so long, you have certainly blossomed into a beauty I did not expect. At the same time I have no wish to marry you, as you have no wish to marry me."

"Then we have no alternative but to try your way so as not to be pestered for the rest of our lives by our fathers. You never know you might easily find someone beautiful and charming who would fit into The Towers and make you a very happy man and give you at least three sons."

Royden laughed.

"I think that is wishful thinking. But, if we tell each other Fairy stories, I now predict that you will find the perfect man who loves you from the moment he sets eyes on you and you will marry each other and be very very happy."

"That is exactly what I want," Malva said. "Who knows we may both of us find what we are seeking while we are travelling under such pretence and I will dance at your wedding with the greatest delight."

"And I will give you a present you have always wanted, but which you had always found too expensive to buy," Royden boasted.

Then they were both laughing because it sounded so absurd.

Then he said,

"I think the sooner we set off on our secret journey, the better. At the same time we must make a date when we will break it to our fathers that we are married. Then I can have the yacht waiting for us near the House of Lords. We will then slip away before they realise what has happened."

"Do you really think they will keep silent?" Malva asked. "It would be terrible if they talked and we came back to find everyone smiling at us and a whole pile of presents waiting for us to write letters of thanks for!"

Royden thought for a moment.

"I think if we are both firm about how shocked the Queen would be at you degrading your mourning, so to speak, neither father would breathe a word to anyone."

Malva thought that this was certainly true of her own father.

He would hate to upset the Queen, who was always sending for him and there was no doubt at all that Her Majesty would be very shocked if she thought that Malva was breaking all her strict rules of mourning.

"From the way she dresses," Royden said, "I expect that she will mourn Prince Albert until she dies. It will undoubtedly be the longest mourning that has ever taken place on earth!"

Malva laughed because it sounded so funny.

Then she said,

"I think that we are taking a desperate leap into the dark. Equally I cannot see any alternative except to hear your father and mine either begging or ordering us to obey them."

"That is just what I think myself," Royden replied. "You know as well as I do that my father can be most obstinate when he sets his mind on anything and is then determined that it shall be done his way."

"Papa is just the same. I love him dearly, but, as he always knows best for other people, he thinks that this is best for me. I cannot think of any other way in which we will manage to escape being tied to each other for the rest of our lives."

"You must not think it rude," he said, "when I say that this is the one situation I wish to avoid. I had no idea when this inspiration came to me like a flash of lightning that you would be sensible enough to accept it."

"I think it is very clever of you to come up with a solution," Malva said. "I lay awake last night and I could not think of any way without hurting and upsetting Papa and practically being turned out of the back door that I could escape from marrying you."

"I felt just the same," Royden confessed. "In fact I thought that my life of freedom had come to an end and I was to be imprisoned for the rest of my life!"

Malva laughed.

"We have to play our parts very cleverly. It is going to be difficult, but not half as difficult as it would be to pretend we were happy when we were not happy at all."

"I think you are absolutely splendid in accepting my idea, Malva. I take my hat off to you. The only thing we both have to do is to act our parts so well that neither of our fathers, who are both very intelligent men, realise that the whole scenario is a farce."

"Of course you are right there," Malva answered. "I promise you I will act my part with an unquenchable enthusiasm because at the end of it I will be free."

"That is exactly what I want too. I can assure you that I will be single for many, many years and you will doubtless be grey before I finally marry and produce the heir they make so much fuss about."

He spoke with so much conviction in his voice that Malva could only laugh.

"You have forgotten," she said, "it is not you who produces an heir but the lady who will be your wife."

"I can only hope," Royden replied, "that you will still dance and even sing at my wedding."

"I expect by the time it takes place I will be too old to do so. But I will certainly give you a present."

"For that, of course, I will be very grateful."

They were both laughing as they left the Pavilion and walked back to their horses.

As they reached them, Royden said,

"I will make all the details absolutely clear and arrange for the yacht to be ready and waiting for us when we reach London."

"Is anyone staying at The Towers this weekend?" Malva asked.

"No one I have heard of."

"Then I suggest you ask my father and me to have dinner with you on Sunday night, but, of course, with no other guests present. It is then, after dinner you produce the Special Licence you spoke about and we tell them that, to avoid being talked about and, of course, upsetting the Queen, we are leaving for London and will be setting out from the Thames as soon as the deed is done."

"That is an excellent idea," Royden said. "Thank you for thinking of it."

As an afterthought he added,

"By the way pick up your clothes when we leave The Towers and, as we will be on the sea and in a part of the world where we are unknown, for Heaven's sake don't bring anything with you that's black! I am sick to death of the colour and it is only by a miracle that it is being of use to us now."

"We hope it will be. So cross your fingers that we are not boasting too soon, Royden."

"I want to wave my hat and shout from the roof tops that we have solved the most difficult problem any two people have ever faced with," he chuckled.

As he spoke, he helped Malva onto her horse.

"I can only pray we will not be found out," Malva answered, "and will return in one piece at the beginning of August when my mourning will be over."

"We will certainly be in mourning if we fail and they find out that we were lying! What a blessing it is that the horses cannot talk."

"They are the only ones to know our secret," Malva smiled.

She paused for a moment to add,

"I am quite certain that we are being bright enough to win the battle even before it has even begun."

She moved forward as she spoke.

And, as she rode away, Royden lifted his hat.

He patted his horse before he mounted and said,

"That is a very clever woman, Solomon, and you can take it from me that they are few and far between."

CHAPTER THREE

As she reached her home, Malva started to pack her pretty coloured clothes that had been put away when she was plunged into black.

She also found some dresses of her mother's which had been packed away neatly in the wardrobe, but had not gone out of date.

They were the dresses she had worn at the Hunt Balls in the winter and the Garden Parties in the summer.

As they were all the same size, Malva thought that they might well be useful to her on the voyage.

Anyway if no one else enjoyed the pretty colours, Royden would certainly do so.

She felt that they were doing something extremely dashing and unexpected.

At the same time she was still really terrified that she might have to marry someone she did not love.

In a small way she had seen how disastrous these arranged marriages could be.

There were people in the village who never stopped quarrelling and there had been a case where the doctor had knocked down his wife. She had injured herself when she fell and everyone had talked about it and said how they were always arguing and he was at times brutal towards her.

She did not, however, think that Royden would be anything like that doctor.

But she knew only too well from the gossip, which had been continuous ever since he had grown up that he had pursued beautiful women with whom he was reported to have had an *affaire-de-coeur*, but they did not last long.

Almost before Malva had heard about one beauty, her place was taken by another who was reputedly even lovelier.

'If I had a husband who would behave like that,' she thought, 'I would be utterly and completely miserable.'

She thought too that Royden, if she was forced to marry him, would look down on her because her father was not of the same rank as he was.

It would always give her a feeling of inferiority.

At the same time Royden's intriguing plan seemed rather ingenious, but she hated having to lie.

She could remember only too well her old Nanny saying to her,

"Tell the truth and shame the Devil."

While her mother had said,

"Never lie, darling, it is very degrading. Also it is very wrong."

Malva had therefore always tried to tell the truth even though at times she was tempted to evade it.

Yet the one excuse for Royden's method of saving them from being tied to each other was that they were not hurting anyone except themselves.

Certainly, according to him, it was preventing his father from threatening to die.

She did not honestly think that the Earl was as ill as he pretended to be, but he was a man who always had his own way and expected everyone to obey him instantly.

So it was really sensational for him to be opposed by his son and to have to listen to endless arguments as to why he did not wish to marry and produce the expected heir.

'I know that the Earl is terrified that the family will come to an end,' Malva thought, 'all the same there is still plenty of time for Royden to marry and eventually he will find someone he loves who is not already married.'

She realised that she was trying to put not only a viable explanation but a coloured blanket, so to speak, over the part they were prepared to act.

But she thought it was something that they could both do with a clear conscience, simply because to walk deliberately into a black pit of unhappiness was wrong and incredibly foolish.

When she had packed three trunks of her clothes, she hid them in a room that was not often used and locked the door.

She did not want the servants to be curious as to what she was doing, as she knew only too well that in the village nothing went unnoticed and everything was talked about at great length.

Her father was very busy at the moment as he was building a new farm on the edge of the estate where it joined with the Earl's.

He intended to breed a new type of sheep that had been very successful in other parts of the country and the project certainly took his mind off his daughter and the troubles being caused by the Earl.

Thus it was quite a surprise when Lord Waverstone received a note from his Lordship asking if he and Malva would have luncheon with them the following day.

'It's rather funny he asked us to luncheon,' Malva thought. 'I should imagine that dinner would be far more convenient, when Papa has finished inspecting the farms and the estate and I would be able to ride for much longer than I could do if I have to change my clothes in order to go to The Towers.'

There was, however, no point in her complaining about this aloud because the messenger from The Towers was waiting for an answer.

"Say we will be with him as he asks at a quarter-to-one," her father suggested. "I wonder if there will be a party."

This question was quickly answered when half-an-hour later Malva received a letter from Royden.

It was very short and read,

"*Join me on horseback at nine o'clock tomorrow morning. You can guess where we are supposed to go.*"

Malva read the letter several times.

She wondered what he meant by the last line.

Eventually she came to the conclusion that it was something to do with their supposed marriage.

She was still pondering if she was wrong in taking part in the subterfuge even if it was intended to save herself and Royden from what they both knew would be a life of unhappiness.

But she did not think that she should be riding if they were pretending to get married.

However she was soon to be disillusioned.

Because she thought that they might be lunching at The Towers before she had sufficient time to change, she put on her best and most attractive riding habit which she thought was too good to be used in the country.

She took a little more care than usual in arranging her hair so that she looked not only smart but extremely pretty when she rode to where Royden was waiting for her.

It was on the edge of the same wood that bordered their two estates.

Royden was looking very smart and he raised his top hat as she joined him.

"What is happening and why are we meeting here?" she asked him.

"Because we are supposed to be married by now," he replied. "I am glad you are looking so pretty and as you see I am dressed as fashionably as I dared to be for such an important confrontation."

Because of the way he spoke, Malva laughed.

Then he said,

"It's no laughing matter. We have to carry this out with brilliance and intelligence. Otherwise we might be defeated and find ourselves bound together forever by a golden ring."

"We certainly want to avoid that," Malva replied. "But you have not told me where we are going."

"We are actually going to ride to the far end of the estate and stay there until it is time to return for luncheon where our fathers will be waiting."

He paused for a moment before he added,

"Doubtless they will be discussing the enormous number of presents we will be receiving and the fireworks which are to be set off at night to make sure that the stars appreciate us as much as the villagers and the others who will be watching them on the lawn at The Towers."

Malva laughed.

Then she said,

"I do hope we are not caught out in this. We will look very stupid if they realise that we are acting out a lie."

"We must avoid that at all costs," Royden replied. "Now come along. I suggest that we ride towards the lake and then cut down into the large wood and hide where no one will find us."

As it all seemed absurd and almost childish, Malva laughed again.

But she realised that she and Royden would be in deep trouble if their parents suspected that they were being deceived.

"What have you done," she asked as they rode off, "about the marriage documents that you thought you could obtain?"

"I have them," he answered. "There is a Chapel in Mayfair where people are still married without a Special Licence."

"Oh, yes, I have heard about it. Did you go there?"

"No, I obtained a Special Licence that can be used in our own private Chapel at The Towers," he replied.

"I had forgotten about that. Because it is never open, which I would so like it to be, I was not aware that people could be married there."

"If I ever do marry, I will be married in the Chapel where I was actually Christened," Royden said.

Malva had often thought it was a pity that, after his wife died, the Earl had put her body in the family vault and closed the Chapel door so that no one could go into it

She remembered as a small child being taken there and thinking how pretty the Chapel was with its coloured glass windows and very beautiful altar.

Now she thought it was very sensible of Royden to want to be married in his own Chapel rather than a Church which seemed much less personal than if it was part of the great house.

"What did you find?" she asked aloud.

"I found two printed forms that are given to people who are married there. On them are printed the words,

"The Chapel to Saint Michael and All Saints at Hillingwood Towers."

Malva was listening intently and was about to ask what they should do about it when Royden went on,

"I cleverly erased that inscription and left a blank so that when my father asks me, which he obviously will, where we were married we will say it is a secret because no one must know we have been married until later when we return and announce our marriage to the world."

"So we now have two forms saying we are legally married and signed by a Priest," Malva said as if she was thinking it over.

"Actually they were signed by me," Royden said. "But I have put in a name that sounds not only clerical but someone of high rank in the Church hierarchy as if he was a Canon."

He spoke so seriously that Malva could not help laughing.

"You certainly do these sorts of things thoroughly," she said. "I am sure most people would not have thought of anything so complicated."

"We have to be quite certain that our fathers are convinced we are actually joined in wedlock," Royden told her. "So that it will be an even greater shock when we tell them we want a divorce!"

"In real life it would be an outrage that they would never allow," Malva murmured.

"It is something they could not prevent," Royden answered. "I have gone into this matter thoroughly and if two people really want to have a divorce and, as you know, it would have to go through Parliament and would prove expensive, there is no doubt that it would be impossible for anyone to stop them doing so."

Malva thought that, because it would cause a great deal of adverse gossip besides being printed in every paper, she was quite certain that the Earl and her father would do everything in their power to prevent it.

When they eventually found it was all unnecessary and they were not married after all, it would be quite obvious that they would feel relieved rather than angry at her and Royden at being deceived.

At least she hoped so.

They rode on through a field and then dipped down into the leafy wood and finished up looking over the wild undeveloped part of the County.

"No one will see us here," Royden suggested. "So we may as well enjoy the ride while we have the chance."

"I am delighted to do so," Malva agreed. "I seldom have the opportunity of going so far from home. We could not ask for a sunnier day."

"Everything is in our favour. So we must be very careful not to make a mess of things."

"I am quite prepared to let you do the talking," Malva said. "I will merely look goofy and say nothing!"

Royden laughed.

"You look very pretty and that is more important than making remarks that afterwards you might wish you had not said."

"That is exactly what I am afraid of. We have to be convincing otherwise all this will be in vain and we will be back arguing day after day and night after night as to why we have no wish to be husband and wife."

"It is impossible for both of us. By the way I have done something rather clever, Malva, that I think you will approve of."

"What is that?" she asked a little nervously.

In fact she could not help wondering what else he was going to spring on her.

"I have just bought," he announced grandly, "a new yacht."

"A new yacht!" Malva exclaimed. "But you have only had your other one for two years."

"I know that," he replied, "but I thought it would be a mistake to hide in it for the simple reason that at least two of my yachtsmen have relations in the village – "

" – and they might talk," Malva finished for him.

"Of course they will. They will be thrilled that two people they know so well have been married. Naturally their mothers and fathers and half a dozen of their friends will want to know where we are spending our honeymoon and if we are supremely happy as they will be certain we are."

"I did not think of that," Malva admitted. "You are clever. But it must be a tremendous extravagance for you to buy another yacht."

"Actually it was not as expensive as I expected it to be. It is French and has a French crew."

"You really are very astute!" Malva exclaimed. "I should never have thought of that. So, of course, they will not be especially interested in you and me as those working on your other yacht would be."

"Exactly. And I have already told them that I will be travelling with my sister."

"I feel I should curtsey to that, but it's impossible to do it when I am riding side-saddle!"

"I will accept your compliment without any extras attached to it!" Royden smiled.

While they were talking, they had travelled some way into the wilder part of the countryside.

Because the sun was hot Malva insisted on riding into a small group of trees for shade and Royden agreed with her.

Dismounting, he let his horse drink at the stream that was running through the copse.

Malva felt that she should do the same and took her horse there as well.

Then they sat down on a fallen tree and discussed how long their supposed honeymoon should take.

"What is much more important than anything else," he said, "is to make it absolutely clear to our fathers that they must, on no account, tell anyone we are married or where we have gone."

"I know," Malva agreed. "But you must give them an alternative answer to the obvious questions they are then bound to ask."

She hesitated for a moment before she added,

"Your friends in London will surely be wondering what has happened to you. While I don't suppose anyone in the country will be in the least curious as to why I have disappeared."

"I think my father will prefer to stay here in the country and it is only yours who will be bombarded as you say with questions and find it difficult to answer them."

"I am sure he will be intelligent enough to keep people from being too curious," Malva replied. "And you know how many people Papa sees one way or another at his meetings and in his Club."

"Your father is indeed certainly a most intelligent gentleman whom I have always admired. I think that we can trust him not to confide in anyone."

"I hope so," Malva sighed. "Otherwise it will be very difficult for both of us when we return."

"Everything is difficult whichever way we look at it. More than anything else our real difficulty will be to make them fully aware that we have absolutely proved that marriage is quite impossible for both of us and therefore we have to remain single."

He stopped for a moment before he added,

"At least I have to."

"So do I," Malva countered. "I am determined not to marry until I fall in love. I will certainly not have the opportunity of doing so when we are sailing over the seas to a strange and not at all well-known country with only you and your French crew to talk to."

"You sound as if you think it will be very boring."

"On the contrary, I am looking forward enormously to seeing parts of the world I would never be able to see if you did not take me there. I am certain that we will find all sorts of dramas that we could never even imagine."

*

They sat talking on in the copse until it was twelve o'clock.

Then they rode quickly back to The Towers.

Their fathers were sitting expectantly in the study.

Each had a glass in his hand as Royden and Malva entered.

"Oh, here you are!" the Earl exclaimed. "I was just beginning to wonder if you had forgotten we were having luncheon today."

"No, we have not forgotten, Papa," Royden said. "And, as I am sure you will agree, this is a very important occasion."

The two elderly men looked at them questioningly.

Then Royden continued,

"You wanted us to be married and you, Papa, made it quite clear that I was not only upsetting you but I was killing you because I would not do so."

The Earl said nothing, but frowned as his son went on,

"We also believed that, however much you begged us to do so, it was impossible for us to get married until Malva had come out of her period of mourning because, as no one knows better than Lord Waverstone, Her Majesty the Queen would be horrified at us breaking her rules especially where I am concerned as I am her Godson."

Malva, who had forgotten this, looked at him in surprise but said nothing.

Then he carried on,

"We have therefore, because I am worried about your health, Papa, and the feeling of uncertainty Malva and I have caused you both, been married secretly in a Chapel where we were not forced to produce a Special Licence."

Both fathers sat up and stared at Royden as if they could not believe their ears.

Lord Waverstone spoke first.

"You have been married!" he exclaimed. "I don't believe it!"

"I have two documents to prove it," he replied. "But as you will understand it is absolutely imperative that no one, and I mean no one, including the servants, should realise that this ceremony has taken place. If it does and Her Majesty hears about it, she will be extremely annoyed and particularly because I happen to be her Godson, I will be in disgrace and so will you, Papa."

"So will my father," Malva joined in. "He is often at Windsor Castle and no one knows better than he how the

Queen expects to be obeyed implicitly especially when it concerns marriage."

Both the elderly men seemed for the moment to be shocked into silence.

Then Royden carried on,

"What we plan to do, my wife and I, is to go abroad immediately for our honeymoon. It will then be up to Lord Waverstone to convince everybody that Malva is staying away with her friends preferably in the North where they cannot be in communication with them. We will not return home until Malva is no longer in deep mourning and it is then that you can begin to plan the firework display and all the other festivities you connect and, quite unnecessarily I may say, with marriage."

"And you were really married in this extraordinary way?" the Earl asked.

Royden handed him the two forms which he had shown to Malva.

He looked first at one and then the other.

Then he exclaimed,

"This does not say where the marriage took place!"

"As you can see, I have arranged it," Royden said, "just in case the forms are left lying around and someone takes the trouble to see if we really went there and asked questions as to where we have gone."

He paused for a moment before resuming,

"I have no wish for anyone to hear of our marriage and least of all to know where we are on our honeymoon. You know that Her Majesty would think it exceedingly wrong of us to have disobeyed her orders. I have no wish when we return to find that we are barred from Windsor Castle!"

"I am sure you will never be," Lord Waverstone said. "At the same time I think it is extraordinary of my daughter to get married in such an odd manner and without my being present."

Malva went to his side.

"You would have argued, Papa, against us doing so. But you know as well as I do that if you kept talking about us getting married it would leak out sooner or later. Then there would be too many curious people for us to be able to keep it a secret."

"But we meant you to have a very large Reception here," the Earl said. "In fact, Arthur and I were talking it over before you arrived."

"That is exactly what I was afraid of," Royden said. "As you well know everyone has ears in this place where it concerns you and me. It would only be a question of time before the gossips in London would be chattering behind their hands. The fact that we were to be married would be no longer a secret, but doubtless anticipated with glee in every newspaper."

There was silence around the room.

Then after a moment he continued,

"Malva was very anxious, if we did marry, to have a very quiet wedding as her mother could not be present and I was concerned that, as Papa was worrying himself over it so much, he might make himself really ill and that has to be avoided at all costs."

He thought as he spoke that his father looked rather guilty because of his exaggerated play of ill health when they had discussed his marriage earlier.

"What Malva and I are determined about," Royden went on, "is that, when we do return, you give us time to breathe before we have a large wedding party here with, of course, fireworks for the villagers and barrels of drink for those who are working on the land."

He spoke almost scornfully as he added,

"Then all of those who are curious will come to stare at my bride and those who chatter too much will give you a list of the ladies who will be disappointed that now I am a married man."

The Earl laughed as if he could not help himself.

"I am quite certain there will be plenty of those," he agreed, "all the more reason why you should get rid of them in one fell swoop and then they will have nothing to talk about for some time."

"When is all this to take place?" Lord Waverstone wanted to know.

"As soon as we return, but I cannot tell you at the moment exactly when that will be. We are going to explore a little of the world I have not seen for several years and which will be something new and intriguing for Malva."

He paused for a moment before he said,

"All you have to do in our absence is to explain that we are on holiday with friends, but not mention the word 'marriage' until we actually meet up with you again in this room."

There was more silence.

Then, after a while, the Earl said,

"Well, you have certainly taken my breath away. This is something I never expected."

"Nor did I until you put the idea into my head," his son replied. "If you are both shocked and surprised, then just remember that it is a complete and absolute secret and no one must know, however curious they may be, what has really happened."

Lord Waverstone chuckled.

"I might have guessed, Royden, that you would do something original. This is certainly a novel way of setting out on the biggest enterprise any man could take in his life – and that is marriage."

"And particularly when he has a father," Royden said, "who persuades him it is essential that it should take place immediately. That is indeed exactly what Malva and I have done."

"I thought I should be blamed sooner or later," the Earl remarked. "As I said, you have taken my breath away and this is something I never expected even in my wildest dreams."

Royden glanced at the clock on the mantelpiece.

"Luncheon should be ready now," he said. "I told the servants when I came back to the house that we would go into the dining room when we were ready as I had a few matters to discuss with my father before we did so."

"Then we will go into luncheon," the Earl agreed, "and I suppose not one word of what has happened here must be discussed at the table."

"As I have said already," Royden asserted, "there are ears everywhere and tongues who want to chatter about us. What Malva and I have done this morning must not be mentioned to anyone until we return from our honeymoon. Incidentally we are leaving for London as soon as luncheon is finished."

Lord Waverstone put his hand up to his forehead.

"I cannot believe this is really happening," he said.

"I agree with you," the Earl sighed. "I have never known the ceiling fall in when I least expected it."

"Well, just think about it, Papa," Royden said, "you have achieved exactly what you asked for, only it has come to you in my way rather than yours!"

"You are a most tiresome boy," the Earl replied. "At the same time I must tell you how grateful and how glad I am you that have at last understood the importance of marriage where you are concerned and how delighted I am that the family name will continue for at least, I hope, the next one thousand years."

"I will drink to that," Royden laughed. "But, as I have nothing in my hand, I suggest we all go to the dining room now."

Rather slowly and unsteadily the Earl then rose to his feet and, using his stick, walked towards the door.

Royden waited for Malva to follow.

As she slipped her arm affectionately through her father's, she whispered,

"I want you to be happy, Papa, which I am sure the Earl is."

"I am happier than I can possibly say," he replied. "In fact, my dearest, I am simply and absolutely delighted that you should be married to the one man who thinks the world of you."

Malva drew in her breath.

It then flashed through her mind that she was doing something wrong which would definitely upset her father when he eventually discovered the truth.

Then she told herself it was utterly impossible for her to marry a man who did not love her, someone she thought of just as a good friend and of whom she knew very little.

'We are doing the right thing,' she told herself, as they walked slowly towards the dining room.

At the same time she was doubtful.

*

Luncheon was delicious although the conversation was rather strained as it was impossible for any of them to talk on the subject that was upmost in their minds.

However, when luncheon was over and they moved again into the study, Royden said,

"Now Malva and I are going to London and I hope, Lord Waverstone, that you will stay with Papa until he has adjusted himself to what has happened and will not stay awake worrying when he goes back to bed.

"Of course I will stay with him," Lord Waverstone replied, "and I think we will both discuss your future and, of course, what we will give you as wedding presents when you are prepared to accept them."

"I will accept anything I am offered," Royden said. "And needless to say I would expect the best and the most expensive!"

"That is not the sort of thing that you should say," Malva said reprovingly. "And if you are not careful they will make this an excuse for giving us very small presents, if any at all."

"Well we will leave them to discuss the cheapest they can get away with!" Royden answered.

Malva kissed her father.

"Goodbye, my darling, Papa," she said. "Look after yourself and do be careful that the door of Windsor Castle is still open to us when we return."

"I can only do my best to prevent Her Majesty having the slightest idea that this had occurred," he replied. "I know how she likes being in on a secret before anyone else is aware of it and I can only hope and pray that you will give me just twenty-four hours before your wedding is announced to the world and all and sundry come to know about it."

"I am sure we can arrange that," Malva promised. "So take care of yourself, Papa, and think of me on the high seas and pray that I will not be seasick."

"I will most definitely pray for your happiness, my dearest daughter." her father replied.

He kissed her and so did the Earl.

"I am very proud and delighted to have you as my daughter-in-law," he said. "I know that you will carry on the tradition of this house as one of the most comfortable anyone has ever stayed in."

"I will tell them what was good enough for Queen Elizabeth and a great number of other Royal personages who stayed here in the past is quite good enough for them," Malva replied. "In fact I promise you I will make it good enough for any King or Prince."

"That is what I want to hear, my dear, and I am so delighted that your father and I can join our land and know that our great ambition will be fulfilled when you produce an heir to The Towers and the two estates."

Because they were being deceived, Malva felt not only embarrassed but ashamed.

It flashed through her mind that by being deceitful they would undoubtedly upset the two old gentlemen who had done nothing wrong.

They had merely wanted their family to continue as any member of such august families would desire.

Then she forced herself not to worry about them, but about Royden and herself.

At the same time, when she hugged her father, she whispered,

"I love you, Papa. Look after yourself and pray that I have done the right thing."

As he promised her that he would, she thought that it was going to be difficult to convince herself, as well as her father later, that what she was doing was right.

However, it was no use now, at the last moment, having cold feet.

So she followed Royden to the chaise which was waiting outside.

It was drawn by a team of four perfectly matched chestnuts.

"I will drop Malva off at your house, in plenty of time for the dinner party tonight," Royden said loudly for the butler and footman who were supervising their luggage to hear.

"Yes, I must not be late," Malva replied. "Because it will be a very delightful party and I only wish that Papa and you were coming too."

Lord Wavestone smiled, but did not say anything.

Then, as Royden picked up the reins and the horses started to move, they all waved.

As they then drove along the drive, Malva said to Royden in a whisper so that there was no chance of the groom sitting behind them hearing,

"I feel guilty. It's the biggest lie I have ever told."

"I feel the same," Royden said, "but it's in a very good cause and the alternative is, as you and I have agreed, completely impossible."

"Of course it is, but we have made your dear father very happy and I am just wondering what he will feel when he knows the truth."

"If I know him, he will not fall into a despondency and threaten to die as he did a few days ago. I did not really believe him then. Equally I was afraid to take the risk."

"I understand," Malva said. "I know that it would upset Papa if he had had to argue with me day after day on the same subject and I was determined to go no further."

"I just know we have done the right thing," Royden said. "Although we may well reproach ourselves later, I am more than certain that we have no other alternative at present."

"Only you could have thought of anything quite so different and original to what has ever happened before," Malva sighed.

She paused before she added,

"We can only hope that it will end exactly as you want it to and there will not be the cannonball you might expect."

"Forget it! Forget it!" Royden said sharply. "We might as well relax and enjoy ourselves. We have taken the right decision. It's the only way to make it possible for us to keep our freedom."

"I am sure you are right. It is just something so different from what I have ever done before."

"I might say the same. To tell you the truth, I have never taken any woman on a long journey such as we are undertaking now."

Malva turned her head to look at him.

"Is that correct?" she asked him.

"There is no point in my lying to you. Actually I find it is always better to have a woman in whom I am interested in her own environment. Therefore I do not take an English woman with me to Paris or a French woman back with me to England."

Malva laughed.

"You have certainly thought it all out very adroitly. I can only hope that by the end of our voyage you are not so bored with me that you will want to drown me in the sea!"

"I will try not to do that, but you must also make yourself the perfect companion. To be honest I have not yet discovered one."

Malva stared at him.

"Do you really mean that? In all the journeys you have taken to all sorts of strange places, have you always been alone?"

"Certainly during the voyage. I find beautiful and seductive women in every country I have visited, but they are always best, as I have already said, on their own soil. It has invariably been a big mistake to move them to another place or, as you realise, to take them home with me. I have often thought about them, but have been sensible enough to leave them where they shine the brightest."

Malva laughed.

"I am sure you have it down to a fine art," she said. "But naturally like everyone else I have always wondered why your love affairs end, of course, we talked about them day after day, month after month and never lasted very long."

She thought as she spoke that she was being rather bold, but it was wise to start as she meant to go on.

From all she had heard she was quite certain that he would be very bored with her after a few weeks of being together on his yacht.

"That is the sort of question it is difficult to find an answer to," he replied. "Actually you should not ask it of me."

"If we are to be together for any length of time and there is no chance of you finding any other amusements on board, then it is better for us to be open and frank with each other from the beginning. At least I think so."

Royden chuckled.

"You are right, of course, you are right and it would be a great mistake for you to start off pretending that you are anything else but yourself."

Malva did not speak and he went on,

"Now I think about it I remember that even when you were a child you asked me difficult questions that I found it hard to give an answer to. I expect, as the years have passed, you have not altered."

"It would indeed be polite for me to say that you have grown wiser and in that case more interesting," Malva remarked.

"You are quite right and it is me who should be paying you compliments. But actually I can give you one right away."

"What is that?" Malva asked.

"Well, you are prettier than you have ever been and even prettier than I remember. My job on this journey may be to chaperone you and see that you don't get out of hand with the charming and delightful men we will meet in other countries."

"Now that sounds really interesting and, as I have met very few charming and delightful men in London, I am perfectly prepared to find them abroad which undoubtedly you have been able to do in the past with your ladies."

"Now we are back to me," Royden said, "and that makes me feel rather nervous. I have a feeling that you may know or guess far more than I want you to do."

"Now you are talking nonsense. Because if you have to be careful how I behave and if I know more than you think I know, then it will be impossible for you to be bored. That also applies to me!"

Royden chuckled again.

"For the first time," he said, "I am looking on this as a voyage of discovery and Heaven alone knows what I shall discover about you!"

CHAPTER FOUR

They drove past Buckingham Palace and then were travelling towards the House of Lords where Royden had arranged that his yacht would be waiting for him when he exclaimed,

"I have suddenly remembered I have not told you that we are travelling under assumed names! I am too well known on the Continent and doubtless in Africa as well, that when I arrive I will immediately be pestered by the Embassy and Social people who will want to entertain us. That, as you realise, could be dangerous."

"Yes and, of course, I should have thought of that," Malva replied. "What is your name to be?"

"Because I will forget it if it is not a simple one, I am going to be just Hill, 'Charles Hill'. Charles is actually my other name. And you will be 'Maisie Hill'."

Malva giggled.

"You might have let me choose my own name. I think Maisie sounds rather insipid which I try not to be."

"Which you could never be," the Royden answered. "If you want to change it, you can do so but I have actually put it down in writing for the Captain of the yacht."

"I still think that you might have asked me," Malva retorted. "But I will have to accept 'Maisie' even though it is a name I would certainly not have chosen for myself!"

"Here we go now with our first argument or if you prefer quarrel," Royden joked.

"I expect we will have far worse ones before the trip is over," Malva warned him.

"I sincerely hope not," he replied. "If there is one thing I really dislike it is an argumentative woman who thinks she knows better than me!"

Malva laughed.

"That is one ambition I would never attempt to try for, so I will accept whatever you say mildly and without any argument."

"In which case," Royden replied, "I think that the journey may be very dull."

"You cannot have it both ways," Malva pointed out, "and we will just have to see how things plan out. Of course, if we are to demand a divorce when we get home, it would be a mistake to let every opportunity of aggression pass unnoticed."

"That may be your idea but it's not mine. Ever since I have known you, Malva, which was when you were in the cradle, you have always been extremely pleasant. In fact I cannot ever remember quarrelling with you."

"If you can say that at the end of this journey, it will be a miracle!" she replied.

They were both laughing as he drew up the chaise on the Embankment and Malva could see the top of a yacht through the trees.

"It is here waiting for us," she said excitedly.

"I thought it would be," Royden smiled.

The groom at the back climbed down and ran to the horses' heads.

Royden jumped out and walked to an opening in the Embankment where there were steps leading down to the water.

The seamen from the yacht must have been waiting for him as two of them came hurrying up and he directed them to the back of the chaise where the luggage was.

As Malva reached the ground, he said to her in a quiet voice,

"The sooner we are on board the better, just in case anyone passing by recognises us."

"They will recognise you, not me," Malva replied. "But, of course, you are right we should go aboard and keep out of sight until we sail away."

The Captain was waiting for them at the entrance to the yacht and they were piped on board.

Royden shook hands with him and then turned to Malva,

"Captain Sadoul, let me introduce you to my sister. This is Miss Maisie Hill, who is accompanying me on this expedition."

The Captain bowed politely over Malva's hand and said,

"It's a privilege to have you aboard, *mademoiselle*."

Malva thanked him in fluent French which clearly delighted him.

He replied in the same language so they entered the yacht chattering in French and smiling as they did so.

The yacht was decorated in a very French fashion and it was quite different from any yacht Malva had seen before.

As it happened she had never travelled in one, but had seen several when she had been in London.

The owners of yachts thought it a new idea to have luncheon on board and she had attended one party when they had danced on deck after dinner in the moonlight and thought it all very romantic.

And she wondered if that was what she and Royden might be able to do at some stage on their adventure.

Then she felt that perhaps it might be dangerous, as he travelled so much and he would surely know a great number of people in every country.

It was essential that none of those who he could call friends should meet him with a young woman he said was his sister when they were well aware that he did not have one.

The yacht's Saloon was far more ornate than any English Saloon would be.

When they did sit down for luncheon, Malva found that the French chef had produced a splendid meal that would have delighted anyone who was interested in food.

While they were eating, the yacht began to move slowly away into the middle of the River Thames.

By the time they had finished luncheon they were a long way from London and nearing the English Channel.

"Now I suppose you will want to go below and see your cabin," Royden suggested, as they had finished their coffee.

They were also offered liqueurs, but, while Royden took one, Malva shook her head.

"You might find a liqueur would stop you feeling seasick," he observed sardonically.

Malva laughed.

"I am quite certain I will not be seasick without any additional help."

"If you say that after we have been through the Bay of Biscay, I will be very impressed. I have never travelled there yet with a woman who has not gone to her cabin and refused to say a single word to me until we reached the Mediterranean."

"I hope I will be the exception," Malva smiled.

They went below.

As she expected, Royden took the Master cabin in the stern that had a large double bed in it.

It was decorated with frills which Malva thought, although she did not say so, would have been laughed at by any English Captain.

Her cabin was next door and very prettily decorated with pink chintz and walls that glittered with mirrors and touches of gold paint.

"I feel as if this yacht is already looking at me as if I am a 'plain Jane'," Malva said. "I am sure any English Captain would be shocked at such frivolities as graces your cabin."

"I will let you into a secret," Royden replied. "This yacht was owned by one of the most famous actresses in France. She redecorated it when she bought it and only discarded it because she found that she was always sick at sea. It therefore affected her performance in the theatre."

"She certainly left her original mark on it," Malva said. "I enjoy the prettiness of my cabin and also I am lost in admiration at the decorations in the Saloon."

"Well, at least no one will suspect that we are who we really are. I may tell you that my own yacht when I last took it to the Mediterranean was greatly admired by every country we anchored in."

"I hope one day I will be able to compare the two," Malva remarked.

Then she wondered if she was being rather pushy in suggesting such an idea.

As if he knew what she was thinking, Royden said,

"But we must not forget that when we do return to civilisation it is because we really hate each other and are determined to be divorced so that there will be no question of you going on my yacht until we are at least speaking to each other again in public."

Malva giggled.

"This whole scenario is really quite ridiculous. But it is *your* story and your idea. Therefore I can only hope that I act my part so well that I not only gain the applause of the audience but also yours."

"Well, whatever you may say or think, we will at least be extremely comfortable on this yacht. Although, as you have already pointed out, I may have to redecorate it. I might find it very useful when I want to escape from the chatter of the gossips."

"Let's hope we will give them as little as possible to chatter about."

Malva smiled before she added,

"When I was dancing in London, I used to see them whispering to each other as they sat on the dais. I always wondered who was the victim they were tearing to pieces or dismissing as quite despicable."

"Do they threaten you that much? I must say that they terrify me and I only have to enter a ballroom to know that they were chattering about the lady who accompanied me."

"I suppose they have nothing else to do," Malva said. "The only thing which brightens their days is what they consider bad behaviour on your part and the worse it is the better they are pleased."

"You are absolutely right, Malva. I can imagine only too well what they would say if they knew where we were at this very moment."

"Let's hope that no one is in any way interested in us or wonder where we are until we return to London."

For the moment she spoke seriously.

"You are not to worry yourself," Royden told her. "I am quite certain that no one has the slightest idea that we are not in the country riding amongst the buttercups and concerning ourselves only with country matters."

He paused for a moment before he commented,

"If you ask me, they are actually counting up the *affaires-de-coeur* I have had in the past years and shaking their heads because I refuse to settle down as my father wishes me to do and then produce an heir to follow in my footsteps when I enter the grave."

"You make it sound miserable," Malva answered. "Actually who could not be very happy in such a beautiful house as yours and, of course, it should be filled with the patter of small feet and the nurseries should have children riding on a rocking horse and a nice old-fashioned Nanny knitting by the fireside."

Royden threw up his hands.

"You are now worse than my father," he said. "The answer I have to give you is to enjoy your freedom while you can, as I intend to do, and don't even think of any alternative."

He spoke almost sharply.

And Malva realised that he was not yet at the stage when he could laugh at himself.

'Of course he must settle down and have a family, the bigger the better,' she thought to herself.

She had always thought that The Towers was too large for one man on his own. He should have youngsters racing each other through the corridors and the laughter of shrill young voices pouring out from every room.

Malva's sympathies were with the Earl.

At the same time she had no intention of marrying anyone rich and however important unless she loved him.

'I have to find love,' she mused, 'and perhaps on this voyage when we are running away from marriage, I will find a man who will love me for myself, just as I will love him. Then I will be prepared to marry him however poor he may be and however inconsequential in the Social world.'

She realised that this was something she could not say aloud to Royden.

Therefore, while they toured the rest of the yacht, she made him laugh at everything she had to say about the French influence and the ornate decorations and also the crew who looked very different from what one might have expected of an English crew.

'At least this will give us something to talk about,' she reflected.

She knew if she was honest she would be afraid that the conversation with Royden might lapse and they might well become bored with each other's company long before they could turn round and sail back to England.

Because Royden wanted to go onto the bridge with the Captain after they had looked over the whole yacht, Malva went to her cabin.

Taking off the dress and coat she had travelled in, she lay down on the bed.

It was a very comfortable one and she expected that the mattress had feathers in it rather than rags.

It was quite obvious that the actress who was the previous owner had been determined that her guests should be as comfortable as she herself intended to be.

Malva had put in her luggage, as well as her pretty dresses, several books she wanted to read and she was only hopeful that there would be a library of some sort aboard the yacht.

To her delight there were quite a number of books in the cabin next to the Master one. Granted the majority were in French, but fortunately she could read French as well as English.

Some of them were just romance stories which she usually found were too frivolous to be really interesting.

But there were also, to her delight, some history books of different countries where the yacht had called at one time or another including half-a-dozen in English.

She thought that she would have plenty to entertain her when Royden became disenchanted with her company.

There were some French magazines as well which were amusing if nothing else and she took a selection of books and magazines to her cabin.

It was much later when they were finishing dinner and the Stewards had cleared away everything except the liqueurs Royden was drinking that Malva said,

"I was thrilled to find books aboard the yacht and now you have bought it I think that you should enlarge the library at every Port we stop at."

"That is certainly an idea," he agreed. "Actually I did notice that we had a small library when I was buying the yacht."

He laughed as he added,

"Knowing that you are your father's daughter I was quite certain it was one of the comforts you would require if you were on board for any length of time."

"You are quite right," Malva answered, "and Papa would be the first to agree with you. Actually you may not know that he brought back books with him from every country he visited including several volumes written in the most fantastic languages, which I tried when I was quite young to understand."

"In which case then you will doubtless be able to instruct me on anything I don't know about the countries we will be visiting," Royden replied. "I will, of course, be very grateful to you, Teacher!"

"Now you are making fun of me, but books do make a huge difference in our lives. It would be miserable to be in a strange country of which you know nothing and not have a book to tell you its history and the difficulties it has incurred since it was born, so to speak."

Royden chuckled.

"Now you are frightening me. If you are going to be very erudite, I will jump off at the first Port and go to find some amusing people to travel with us who will make us laugh at the simple things of life rather than the miseries of some strange countries' developments."

"I apologise and I will not preach to you," Malva muttered.

She kept her word and at dinner they laughed at a great number of subjects but nothing too personal.

When she retired to bed, she thought how lovely it was to be at sea and to feel the waves splashing against the side of the yacht.

She knew that tomorrow they might be in the Bay of Biscay and he would laugh at her if she was as seasick as he expected her to be.

'I will show him I am as good a sailor as he is,' she determined as she fell asleep.

*

The next day, as Royden had predicted, the sea was very rough.

The waves were breaking over the bow of the yacht which seemed to have to plough its way through them as best it could.

Malva then ran from side to side to see the waves breaking against the yacht as if it was a toy being tossed from one to the other.

She was fascinated by the scene and the fact that the sun was shining made it all the more absorbing.

When they had luncheon, she loved all the delicious dishes the French chef had cooked for them.

Only when they had finished, did Royden say,

"You are remarkable. I would have bet a thousand pounds that you would have been lying prostrate by now. But here you are enjoying not only the sea but the superb food we have been served."

"Which is delectable," Malva said, "and I would hate to miss any of it."

"At this rate you will eat us out of house and yacht before we even reach Gibraltar!"

"I would hope not, Royden. I have never had such wonderful food as this except in Paris restaurants. Then, as I was much younger, I don't think I appreciated it as much as I do now."

"As we both enjoy France, Malva, I know we will enjoy the French part of Africa. I intend to brush up my French while we are on board, so perhaps we could speak to each other in that language."

"I find that rather depressing," Malva answered. "I like being English, I am extremely proud of being English and although I speak, I am told, very good French, it is always rather an effort. So, quite frankly, I would rather talk to you in my own language."

"I was only teasing," Royden admitted. "I agree with you that it is much easier to be witty and amusing in English than it is in any other language."

"The French would challenge you at that," Malva said, "and they always fancy that their *double entendres* are different to anyone else's."

"I suppose they are. Equally a good English joke, although sometimes rather coarse, is generally amusing."

They argued this statement over a number of other countries.

Malva had to concede in the end that Royden was right and the English, although somewhat rough in many ways, had a wit that was preferable to anyone else's.

"I suppose it is only because we are English that we say so," Malva pointed out. "And we are always eager to grab anything we can from other countries if we only have the chance."

"They try to grab everything they can from us," he countered. "In fact I often think that we are too generous not only with our money and what we grow but with our thoughts and feelings which, of course, are described not only in books but in our speeches."

"I think more important than anything else," Malva said, "is that, when you or my father go abroad, we give people an impression of England which they find hard to forget. I have seen letters Papa has received from other countries and they all admire him enormously, not only for his speeches but because they look on him as a perfect English gentleman."

"A phrase we invented in the reign of King George IV," Royden replied, "who you remember was known as 'the first gentleman of Europe'."

"It is just what we in England have tried to be ever since," Malva said. "What always pleases me is that not only are people like you who are blue-blooded described in that manner. If a shopkeeper or some farmer dies who has always been a good citizen and a man who has kept his word and helped his fellow members, they speak of him as 'a gentleman' and it is exactly what he was."

They talked about many fascinating subjects during dinner and afterwards.

When he went to bed, Royden admitted to himself that he had enjoyed the meal and the company of Malva far more than he had expected to do.

In fact he had thought when he left London that he would, except for the yacht itself, find all the time he spent away dreary and a waste of his time.

Now he told himself to his own surprise that he had enjoyed the conversation at dinner more than anything he had enjoyed for some time.

So he was thinking unconsciously of witty remarks and provocative questions he would ask Malva tomorrow.

*

They stopped at Gibraltar.

Malva was thrilled with the monkeys as any child might be.

She was even more delighted at the many beautiful products that came from Japan which could be bought in the small shops.

Because her father had given her plenty of money to spend on the journey, she bought herself a beautifully embroidered shawl and various other items that came from China including a present for him.

"I have spent a small fortune," she told Royden when they returned to the yacht. "But I am sure that every penny has been a good investment. One day these things which are so lovely will not be on sale anymore."

"Why do you say that?" he asked.

"Because I am afraid that they will be gobbled up by the many grand shops in London, Paris and other Cities.

After all Gibraltar is really only a passing place for ships and will soon be forgotten."

"I suppose you are right," Royden replied. "The *objets d'art* I have brought back from various parts of the world are, in fact, becoming rarer every year."

"I thought when I was walking round your home the other day," Malva said, "the beautiful snuff boxes your grandfather brought back from Russia will, I am certain, now that snuff is no longer fashionable, gradually fade out of existence and we will only have collections like yours where we can admire them."

"I did not think of that before and, of course, you are right," Royden admitted. "My grandfather collected, as you know, special items from all over the world. It is what I am determined to do until I have all I want, which as you say are growing rarer and rarer every year."

"So we must make the best of them while we can," Malva replied. "I beg of you to take me to the Bazaars in the lands we visit that are not overrun by tourists, but are patronised by locals and so are considered very precious."

"I shall enjoy that. In fact I know where there are small out of the way towns which make local products that are bought only by the country people themselves and are seldom discovered by those who merely drop in from other lands."

"Now we have a task that will make our journey far more exciting than it was when you first planned it," Malva enthused.

It passed through Royden's mind that most women would want to talk about themselves and their beauty and they would not be the least concerned with the indigenous products of other countries.

However, as the idea amused him, he proposed,

"I will take you to a place on the coast of Africa, which I found by mistake, but which I think you will find entrancing."

"Why was it by mistake?" Malva enquired.

"Because I was lost and it suddenly began to pour with rain and I wanted somewhere to shelter. As you know rain in Africa is a thousand times more drenching than it is in England."

"I have read that," Malva replied. "Tell me what you found."

"I will take you to it which is far more interesting," Royden told her. "But you will find the products that are made by the local Arabs are not only beautiful but original and completely different from anything you can find in Europe."

"Please don't forget to take me there as soon as you can," Malva urged him. "Because I will then spend all my money and will have to borrow yours!"

"I daresay I will be able to oblige you, but, if I was behaving as I should do with a lady guest, I should be only too pleased to give her anything she may desire however expensive it might turn out to be."

Malva laughed.

"I have always been told that the French beauties are very grasping, but I would expect that really applies to the beauties of every country where you have been talked about by the gossips."

"The trouble with you," Royden said, "is that you know too much about me already while I know nothing about you that I can use as a retort!"

"I am glad about that," Malva answered. "But I am sure you will soon find it easy to hold your own when we come to challenging each other in words and fighting a mock battle with innuendoes!"

Royden smiled.

"Is that what is going to happen?" he asked.

"It always does in books. Although I have not had a chance until now to prove it true, I am quite certain it will be possible."

"If I fight you with words, I might, because you have read so much and speak a number of languages, be the loser and that, as you know, would cause a problem."

"A problem?" she queried.

"Of course, in a proper romantic book the man is always the winner and it is only with love that he comes anywhere close to being defeated because women are so much subtler than he is. And they use everything, however crooked, to get their own way."

"If that is your experience," Malva replied, "I am rather sorry for you. I think women should be attractive but also considerate and, of course, gentle towards the man they love."

She paused for a moment before she added,

"Mama said often enough 'a man must be Master in his own house,' and that, of course, is true. A woman, if she is really feminine wants the man to be the conqueror in every way even though she is clever enough to make him feel that he has to fight for what he really longs for."

Royden stared at her in astonishment.

"Am I really hearing all this from anyone so young and I thought so inexperienced?" he asked.

"You must say it is the right way to look at things if you are a woman," she continued, "and it is only a stupid woman who would fight to get her own way in little things, and lose the most vital one of all – her husband's heart."

She spoke softly.

Royden stared straight at her as if he could hardly believe that she was real.

'How could it be possible,' he now asked himself, 'that someone so young could talk so sensibly about issues that often worry me?'

"Now you are beginning to frighten me," he said aloud.

"Why do you mean?" Malva enquired.

"Because you are talking too intelligently and too sensibly for you to be real. I always thought girls of your age giggled when they talked of love and were concerned only with waiting for a Duke to drop down from Heaven at their feet and ask for their hand in marriage."

"That is what they hope will happen. The girls at school and those I spent my time with when I first left my home always talked about men just as if they were some strange animal they have to catch and, having caught them, tie them down with a wedding ring so that they could not escape!"

Royden laughed.

"That is exactly what I thought they were doing. I can assure you that is why I ran away from every ambitious mother I could see approaching me and dragging beside her a young girl who was interested, not in me but in my title and, of course, my bank balance."

"Now you are too unkind," Malva replied. "Every girl wants to get married sooner or later and it is always their family who tell them that if they are pretty they must find a man with a title and enough money to keep her in the style that she wants to be kept in."

"Then why are you so different?" Royden asked.

Malva thought for a moment as if she was choosing her words very carefully.

Then she said,

"If I am different, as you say I am, it is because my mother and father were so happy and so much in love that I knew what they felt for each other was something I must feel one day."

She hesitated for a moment before she went on,

"My mother was determined to concentrate entirely on making the house revolve round Papa rather than her. It made him feel important and he admired my mother in a way I find sadly lacking amongst the smart set in London today."

Royden did not speak and she continued,

"They are the women who are unfaithful to their husbands. They run as craftily as they can after someone as handsome and as prestigious as you and are not particularly concerned in turning their home into a place where a man would want to live and linger and be alone with his wife and children rather than with anyone else."

"I can hardly believe you are saying all this," he said. "When you should be thinking, as your father has told you, about getting married yourself and, of course, because he is so aristocratic, having what is known as 'a brilliant marriage'."

"I am only surprised that Papa should agree with your father that you should be married whether you want to or not and that I was the right sort of wife for you," Malva replied.

"How could he possibly know that when I have seen so very little of you?"

"Exactly," Malva agreed. "He was merely looking at it from a Social point of view that I should acquire your title together with the most outstanding and beautiful house in England thrown in for good measure."

"Surely that is what you must have wanted."

"I just knew you would say that," Malva answered. "That is why it must have come as quite a surprise for you when I told you truthfully that I had no wish to marry you."

She paused before she went on,

"Although I have liked you ever since I was a child, I am not the least in love with you and I refuse to marry anyone unless I love him as my mother loved my father and as they loved me in the same way."

She laughed lightly as she added,

"Even if he was the Prince of Wales, I should say 'no' and no one could make me change my mind."

"Except, of course, this miraculous man when you find him," Royden countered slightly sarcastically.

"I am quite certain he is to be found somewhere," Malva replied. "Therefore I will be on the lookout for him on this voyage just as, if you are wise, you will be looking for the perfect woman who is waiting for you somewhere in your life although you have not yet found her."

"The perfect woman exists, I am quite certain, only in my imagination. Although I have hopes I might find your magical man for you in the middle of the desert or on top of a mountain. But I think perhaps that both of us are dreaming dreams which will never come true."

"But they have to," Malva cried. "Because we are clever we will find what we are seeking and I am quite certain that the beautiful lady you will love is, at this very moment, looking up into the sky and praying that God will send her the man of her dreams."

She spoke in a soft voice that was almost hypnotic.

Royden then stared at her again until he said almost abruptly,

"I only hope you are right, Malva, but the betting is one hundred to one against us finding anything of the sort on this voyage or indeed anywhere else."

"The unexpected often happens when we are quite certain that it is unobtainable. Therefore, while you go on sneering at the idea, it may creep up beside you when you least expect it and I will go on wishing on the stars and I am certain that one day the man I am dreaming about will drop down on me from Heaven."

There was silence for a moment.

Then Royden broke it,

"In which case I will wish you good luck and good hunting, but I would not mind betting that we will both go home empty-handed."

Malva did not speak for a moment.

Then she said with a twinkle in her eyes,

"As I don't want to lose any of my money, I will not accept your bet!"

CHAPTER FIVE

The sun was shining and the sea was glittering with its rays.

As they proceeded slowly down the coast of Africa, Royden insisted that they should stop at small bays where they could swim.

"I love the sea," he said. "But, of course, you need not join me unless you really want to."

Malva smiled at him.

"I enjoy the sea too," she asserted. "I will race you the first time we find a place to do so."

Royden thought that she was boasting.

He was most surprised when they had anchored and she began diving straight off the yacht into the sea.

He had been astonished when Malva appeared in a rather pretty bathing suit, but with nothing on her feet or her head.

He had never met a woman who was not fussing about her hair when she was at sea.

But Malva dived deeply into the water and came up brushing the curls from her eyes.

Fortunately her hair was not short and when she dried it, it looked as pretty as it had been when they left London.

They then raced each other in the sea.

But Malva insisted that Royden should give her a good start.

"It's only fair," she said, "because I am not only a woman but also smaller than you and so have to take more strokes than you do."

Royden could not argue about that.

But while he expected to beat her easily, he found that he had to exert himself to keep up with her and then to win at the last moment.

She laughed when he did so and observed,

"You would be very annoyed with yourself if you lost to a woman and you will never be quite certain if I had allowed you to be the victor or if you really were one."

"That is the most crooked way of putting things I have ever heard," he replied. "I will be very annoyed if you did not acknowledge that I am a superior swimmer at the end of this voyage."

"I will only do that if it is true," Malva answered. "You must remember that, while you have been practising in the sea, I have only had the lake at home to swim in which I admit is very different from the swell that we are enjoying here."

She looked at the sea as she spoke and added,

"I want to pat the waves and tell them that they are making us happy just by moving up against us or carrying us forward with them."

Royden chuckled.

"I have never heard of anyone being affectionate with waves before," he said.

"Then you must know a lot of very silly people," Malva retorted. "The waves are one of the most beautiful sights in the world and I have always thought that we were particularly lucky because we live on an island and the sea, as you know so well, has protected us English from many enemies throughout the centuries."

"I have never thought of it that way," he replied, "but, of course, you are right. It would be a great mistake for us to ever join up with the Continent of Europe and then cease to be an independent nation."

"Exactly. That is what we want to be as we are English, to be able to decide what we will do for ourselves and not be bossed about like so many countries are by their Police or their Royalty."

"Yet we need both," Royden argued, "simply to keep us independent."

"All right, I give in on that point," Malva said. "At the same time the sea is so important to us as a country and I am its most ardent admirer."

She did not wait for Royden to reply, but plunged into the next wave as it rolled towards them.

As he saw it envelop her, he thought that no woman he had ever known could be so totally unselfconscious of her looks.

And at the same time so attractive.

He had to admit that her long fair hair, and it was naturally curly, looked even lovelier when it was rubbed dry after swimming than when it was arranged for dinner in the evening.

He did not say so aloud because he thought, strange though it was, Malva did not expect compliments.

Most women not only expected them endlessly, but demanded them all the time.

As they sailed slowly down the coast, Malva asked Royden,

"Have you been to Dakar before?"

"I have and I hope you will find it as attractive as I did. I thought that we might stop before we actually reach Senegal and take a look at the desert. I went there once several years ago and found a tribe of Bedouin headed by a Vizier who was very hospitable to me."

Melva gave a cry of delight.

"African Bedouin and a Vizier! Oh, please, please let me meet them. I have read so much about them, but never thought I would actually meet them in the flesh."

"Of course you can do so if it interests you," he promised. "They live some way out in the desert, but, if you have never visited a Vizier's house, I am sure you will find it as fascinating as I did and far more comfortable than one expects."

Malva clasped her hands together.

"That is just what I want to see," she said. "I have read about how well their women dance and how they have fought many battles in the desert."

She sounded so enthusiastic and so excited at the prospect of meeting them that Royden went and talked to the Captain.

He knew, as he might have expected, exactly where the Bedouin tribes in that particular part of Africa were to be found.

Also where they could anchor as near as possible to where the Vizier was currently living.

"The tribes move about all the time," the Captain said, "and one never knows where one will see them next. But there is a Vizier who lives near here who has a grand Palace. Everyone who has visited there has told me with awe and admiration how impressed they were with their surroundings."

"And the Vizier welcomed them?" Royden asked.

"Yes, *monsieur*," the Captain replied. "He is much more civilised, I believe, than a number of others and has built himself a Palace which is the admiration of everyone who sees it."

"Then I must certainly take my sister to visit it. It will be easy for her to converse with the Vizier because she speaks fluent French."

"As you do, *monsieur*," the Captain said, "and it is a pleasure to have you aboard."

Royden smiled at the compliment.

He realised that the Captain who was well educated often found the journeys boring unless he had someone who could talk to him fluently in his own language.

He told Malva what he had learnt from the Captain and she was thrilled at the idea of meeting a Vizier and, of course, of seeing where he was living with his tribe.

"I have often thought they must find it trying," she said, "to wander about and have nowhere permanent where they can keep their families."

"You are out of date," the Royden told her. "The modern Bedouin, I am told, likes to settle down if possible in what we would call a 'hamlet'. So the Bedouin Viziers have taken to rivalling each other with the best possessions and naturally the most beautiful women."

Malva laughed.

"I wonder which comes first in their minds?" she mused aloud.

"I am sure you will be able to see that for yourself if the Vizier is kind enough to entertain us, which I am told he will do quite readily, even though we are pretending to be quite ordinary travellers."

"I shall be very grateful for even a little hospitality because I am so curious," Malva replied. "I have just been thinking that one of us should certainly write a book about this delightful journey into the unknown."

Royden smiled.

"You had better keep it for your old age otherwise someone might guess the real reason why it has taken place and that would be disastrous."

"It would indeed," Malva agreed. "I only hope that Papa and your father are not telling anyone at home that we are married."

"I am quite certain we can trust them both. They are well aware that Her Majesty would be furious at you breaking the rules which she had kept herself for years and years and your father, if no one else, is well aware of how she expects to be obeyed by everyone from the smallest to the largest order she gives at Windsor Castle."

Malva laughed.

"They are all terrified of her. I believe, although you seem so cocky about it, that you are frightened too."

"Shall I say I have a great respect for the Royal Family and have no wish to offend them in any way."

"That is a very fine speech," Malva said teasingly. "But, if it came to a crisis, I know you would bow down and obey her command just like everyone else!"

Royden realised that this was more or less true and so he changed the subject.

*

They reached an enchanting little bay that night and anchored as close as they could to the land so that the yacht was hardly moved at all by the waves.

Malva woke early.

Putting on her bathing dress she ran up on deck and as she half-expected Royden was already there climbing into the water.

"We had better not dive here," he said, "as it is not very deep and you might find yourself hitting your head on the bottom."

"I think that is unlikely. However I will not take the risk, Royden."

She followed him down the rope ladder and then jumped into the water.

With the sun glinting on her golden hair she looked, Royden thought, like a mermaid as she swam out to sea obviously thrilled by the waves and the sunshine.

She swam so fast that it took him a considerable amount of effort to catch up with her.

Then she turned round smiling and called out,

"This is wonderful! I have never enjoyed a holiday more."

"I admit we are very lucky with the weather and the attention we receive from the French sailors on my new yacht," he replied.

"I thought at first that you were very extravagant," Malva said. "But now I think you have made an excellent purchase and, even though it was expensive, it is obviously cheap at the price!"

Royden laughed.

Then he said,

"I want you to enjoy Africa which I have always found most attractive. I have already told the Captain that we want to go ashore and he will organise a conveyance which will take us out into the desert."

"Oh, you are kind!" Malva exclaimed. "I want to do that so much, but I did not want to pressure you."

"I assure you that I am not being pressured and I will enjoy it just as much as you do," Royden replied. "I suggest we have luncheon early and then drive out into the desert. We will then see if my friend the Vizier is still in residence. He was certainly in excellent form five years ago when I last visited him."

"I cannot wait to make the acquaintance of a real Vizier," Malva said excitedly. "So I will swim back to the yacht to make myself look presentable as, of course, you would expect your sister to be."

She did not wait for him to answer, but swam off at a tremendous pace until she reached the yacht.

As she climbed up the rope ladder, she saw that Royden was following her but not hurrying in any way.

She was thinking that he had done all this before and it was not as exciting for him as it was for her.

But she was exceedingly grateful to him for doing what she wanted even though it was nothing new where he was concerned.

Because she thought it was very necessary for her to look her best, she put on one of her prettiest summer gowns and arranged her hair neatly on top of her head.

She felt that a hat would look out of place amongst the Arab women who never wore one and, should the sun be very strong, she had a pink sunshade to protect her from burning.

Luncheon was a quick meal that they ate without talking very much because their conveyance, which was a very strange-looking vehicle drawn by two horses, arrived before they had finished the first course.

"I am afraid you will not be very comfortable," the Captain said when he told Royden that it was waiting for him. "But most people in this part of the world journey only on their feet and it was the best they could provide at a moment's notice.

"I am sure it will take us to where I want to go," Royden said. "My sister has never seen the desert before and that in itself will be an experience for her."

"Of course it will, *monsieur*," the Captain agreed. "At the same time I should take two cushions to sit on as there are a great number of stones in the sand round here."

They did as the Captain suggested and the moment luncheon was finished they drove off.

The horses were rough-looking but fast.

When they reached a more sandy part of the desert the cart or carriage, or whatever they called it, was not really as uncomfortable as Royden had feared.

There was a cover over the part where they were seated and at first Malva thought it unnecessary.

Then, as the sun in the afternoon grew stronger and hotter, she found the protection it gave her was something she really needed.

They drove across the desert with nothing to break the sand and the streams they passed occasionally were not large enough to give any floridity to the landscape.

They must have driven on for nearly two hours and had said very little to each other.

Royden was intent on driving the horses as fast as he wished them to go and, after a few more miles, Malva gave a little cry.

"Look! Look ahead!" she exclaimed.

"You are right," he replied. "That is the Vizier's Palace. As you see there are other small houses round it so that it is a permanent building to which, however far he journeys across the desert, he inevitably returns."

"I expect the Bedouin to be always on the move," Malva said. "I never imagine them settling down in what I can see now is a small village of their own."

"I think my friend here has been inspired because the Sultan, who is the Head and Leader of them all, has a magnificent Palace a long distance from here, which I am sure is so magnificent that it's the envy of every member of the Bedouin tribe."

Malva was listening intently, but her eyes were on the buildings that they were rapidly approaching.

As they drew nearer, she saw that there was one large building and the rest were very small and gave the impression of not being particularly well-made.

But the Vizier's Palace was markedly different.

The tall building was bristling with high crenelated ramparts from which a massive tower protruded.

After they had passed through the gates which led to it and proceeded up the narrow passage to what Royden said was the main doorway, she could see that the Palace itself was well constructed and massive.

It was completely different from anything Malva had expected.

She looked round her with delight, feeling that this was something she would always remember and would tell her father about when she returned to England.

They stopped the carriage and then Royden helped Malva to the ground.

A huge wooden brass-studded door was opened and a number of white-robed men ran out to wave excitedly at what they clearly believed were important visitors.

Now Malva could see a long succession of twisting galleries off which she had an occasional glimpse of square courtyards and fountains.

They were escorted through a labyrinth of twisting passages filled with men, children and animals.

Finally they reached what Malva guessed was the centre of the Kasbah and imagined it was where the Vizier must live.

Malva was amazed after looking at the windowless exterior of the Kasbah to find that inside it was more like a Palace.

They walked over the finest mosaic floors and the walls were covered with carved arabesques and tiles of the most intricate patterns in many brilliant colours.

The tall ceilings were of richly painted wood while columns of carved capitols separated some of the rooms beside screens of lacework.

Finally they were taken into a large room where multi-coloured High Atlas rugs from the North covered the floors and there were silk embroidered hassocks of red, green, white and yellow, all made of goatskin.

A silver lantern was suspended from the ceiling.

As they stood in the centre of the room waiting, exquisitely embroidered curtains were thrown aside and a man came through them.

He was elderly with a short white beard and he was wearing in his belt a jewelled dagger carved in precious stones, which proclaimed his rank.

For a moment he just stood looking at Royden, then he walked towards him and, holding out his hand, said in French,

"Let me welcome you, *monsieur*, and I think I am right in believing that you own the yacht that anchored in the bay last night."

"You are right, Your Excellency," Royden replied in French. "I am Charles Hill and I have brought my sister, Maisie, to meet you as one of the most important people in this whole area."

The Vizier bowed at the compliment.

Indicating some brightly coloured hassocks beside him, he suggested,

"Let us sit down and talk."

The Vizier settled himself on the largest and most colourful hassock with a lattice-work background behind it.

Servants appeared with sweet mint tea in handleless cups and trays of sweetmeats which were made of almonds and honey.

Malva sipped the mint tea.

Only as the servants withdrew did the Vizier look towards her somewhat curiously.

"My sister and I," Royden said in French, "are very interested in the magnificence of your Kasbah."

"I am glad that you have come to visit me," the Vizier replied.

They ate the sweetmeats the servants had presented to them and the Vizier began to talk to Royden about the difficulties they had endured during the winter.

He then asked him questions about his yacht and the speed it travelled at.

After only a short time, Royden rose to his feet and thanked the Vizier for his kindness and hospitality.

He said he had visited his predecessor five years ago and was only sorry that he was not here now.

The Vizier then told him that his predecessor, who had been his brother, had unfortunately been killed in a battle with another tribe, who had ventured onto their land and attempted to steal their women.

"I am extremely sorry to hear that," Royden said. "He was very kind to me and I had hoped to enjoy his hospitality as much as I did on my previous visit."

"Then I hope that you will enjoy mine instead," the Vizier replied. "Any friend of my brother's is, of course, very welcome here."

"We will not be staying long," Royden told him. "We are on our way to Senegal, but I know that my sister would love to see more of your beautiful Palace another time."

The Vizier clapped his hands.

Two servants hurried into the room with flowers for Malva and a bag containing fruit for Royden.

Royden then thanked the Vizier for his hospitality and welcome and said that they would call on him again if it was at all possible before they returned home.

"I will be very upset not to see you, *monsieur*," the Vizier replied. "As I have already said, any friend of my brother is a friend of mine."

Because she knew that it was correct, Malva gave him a curtsey and held out her hand.

She thought that he held it a little longer than was necessary.

He looked at her very scrutinisingly with his dark eyes as if he was remembering her face from her eyes to her lips.

Then Royden moved towards the open door.

Malva curtseyed again and followed him.

They were then escorted by the servants in white back to their carriage and the horses, which had been given something to eat and drink, were brought to the door.

As they had walked down the narrow passages with the servants in white in front, Malva had a distinct feeling, although she could not see him, that the Vizier was still watching them closely.

And that in some strange way he still had his eyes on her face.

'I am just imagining it,' she thought to herself.

At the same time she was certain that was what he was doing.

She felt that it was upsetting for some reason she did not understand.

Then they were out of the last gate and driving back over the desert before Royden commented,

"The Vizier's brother was a much more pleasant man. I have a feeling that this one is very different and somehow dangerous."

"I feel the same," Malva said. "But, of course, he could not have been more polite and was apparently glad to see us."

Royden did not answer.

Malva wondered if he was upset at learning of the death of the Vizier he had known.

However, she knew it had been a privilege for her to see the inside of the Vizier's Palace and it was certainly very different from anything she had expected.

The journey back to the yacht was not quite as easy as it had been on the way to the Palace.

The sun had set while they were in the desert.

Now with the swiftness of the change in the sky in the East there were already the first signs of night moving into the sky.

Although Royden drove extremely well, the horses were tired from their outward journey and were therefore slower in returning to the yacht.

It was almost dark when they reached the small bay and saw the yacht below them.

Royden then paid the man who had brought them the carriage.

He was obviously very generous because the man's grateful thanks, expressed in his own language, followed them as they went down the narrow path that led from the top of the cliff to the bay beneath.

There the yacht was waiting with two seamen in charge to row them back to the yacht.

As she climbed aboard, Malva could not help but feel in some way that their visit had not been as successful as Royden had anticipated.

However, she was hot and tired after bumping over the sand for so long

She went to her cabin and, taking off her dress, she lay down for half-an hour on her bed.

The visit was something to remember, she thought, and something she would write about in her diary which she was determined would contain a description of every place they visited.

She had already written short pieces about the other places they had visited or stayed the night in after they had left Gibraltar.

*

When later she went into dinner and found Royden waiting for her, changed as he always did into his evening clothes, she said,

"Thank you so much, Royden, for taking me to that extraordinary Palace this afternoon. I had no idea that anything quite so magnificent would have been constructed in the middle of the desert."

"I thought it would surprise you," Royden replied. "But I was sorry that my friend who had been there when I visited five years ago had lost his life."

He paused before he went on,

"He was considerably more of a pleasant man and was truthful, I believe, when he had said that he admired the English and was so delighted to have me as his English friend."

"You did not tell the Vizier today that you were English," Malva remarked.

"No, I was careful not to betray myself as being anything but who I am pretending to be," he replied.

"Why?" Malva asked.

"Because I thought the moment I first set eyes on him that I did not trust him particularly," he answered. "I suppose it is because I have been so often in the East that I have learnt to be suspicious of anyone and everyone in this part of the world, especially as they are always at war with someone."

He paused and looked thoughtful before he went on,

"Even though my friend had been killed, or so the Vizier said, by an enemy, I would not have been at all surprised if he had not already planned to take his brother's place however difficult it might be."

Malva stared at him.

"Are you suggesting that he deliberately killed his brother?" she asked incredulously.

"I am sure that he would not do anything quite so obvious as that," Royden replied. "Yet he might easily have made it imperative for his brother to fight the other tribe to which, as I am sure you noticed, he did not give a name."

"Now you are making me shiver," Malva said. "I did not think him particularly attractive. But he was very hospitable and I thought that his Palace was fascinating."

"That is just what he meant you to think, yet the moment I saw him I was wishing that his brother was there as I had expected. Although I cannot put it into words, I am sure he is an interloper."

Malva shook herself.

"Now you are scaring me. I have always thought of the desert as a challenge to civilisation because that is what it really is. Yet, when we were driving over it today, I felt that it was safe and free of war and strife as it had never been in the past."

"I assure you that they still take place in this part of the world, but let's forget what happened today and plan what we shall do tomorrow."

"Oh, don't let's move on," Malva pleaded. "It is so lovely here and I am sure that it would be hard to find a bay that makes it so easy for swimming as this one."

Royden smiled.

"I am in no hurry if you are not," he replied. "But I thought, like all women, you are longing to go to the shops and the local Bazaars and buy yourself a lot of unnecessary cargo to return home with."

"Oh, it will not be as bad as that. I will only buy small presents for those who love me and who will be very sad that I am away so long from the festivities that take place in the village at this time of year."

"I suppose that you mean the local cricket match," Royden said, "as well as the annual race meeting which has every sort of race including one for the small children on ponies and donkeys."

"That, I can assure you, is the most popular race of the day. Papa and I always choose the prizes for it and, although you may sneer, the children think that the prizes are every bit as good as if they are receiving the Koh-I-Noor diamond!"

Royden laughed.

"I am sure that is true. We must make sure that, because you cannot be present this year, next year there will be even better prizes both on your part and on mine."

"I will keep you to it," Malva said, "so don't forget your promise when you reach home."

She went up on deck after dinner and stood looking up at the moon which was just coming out in the sky.

There were already some stars glittering overhead and she thought as she had so often how beautiful this part of the world was.

It was then that Royden joined her and said,

"I have been planning with the Captain to take you on another drive tomorrow in the opposite direction. I have something most interesting for you to see there which is very different from all that you saw today."

"Tell me what it is," Malva demanded excitedly.

"No, it is to be a surprise, but I suggest that you go to bed now because it is rather a long journey and I don't want you to be overtired."

"You are making me very curious," Malva said, "and I am longing to know what it is you are going to show me."

"As it is to be a surprise, I am not talking about it anymore until the morning," he declared firmly. "So go to bed and get your beauty sleep and this time tomorrow night you can tell me if I was right or wrong in thinking that you would enjoy it more than anything else on this trip."

"I am already excited and very curious," Malva sighed. "But, as it is so special, I will do as you tell me and go to bed."

She drew in her breath before she added,

"Thank you, thank you for today. It was thrilling and something I will write down in my diary so as not to forget any of it."

"It will be a book we will have to publish when we get home," Royden replied. "I am sure it will be a great success and the people who have never visited this part of the world except in their dreams will find it fascinating."

"I will make it seem very very real to them so that they will not feel forgotten," Malva answered.

As Royden did not answer, she walked away.

"Goodnight," she called back, "and if you don't dream of that Palace, I am quite certain I shall."

She did not hear Royden's reply.

But she heard him laughing as she ran down the companionway to her cabin.

CHAPTER SIX

The following day was a disappointment.

Royden was informed quite early that the carriage he had ordered was not available until the following day.

So when Malva came down to breakfast, he told her that they would have to postpone their special visit for at least twenty-four hours.

"I am very sorry," he said.

Malva smiled.

"I don't mind. This is the best place I have ever known for swimming and I was thinking last night when I went to bed that I would rather swim than sightsee."

"This is something quite new," he replied. "You had told me you only wanted to examine statues, Churches, Palaces and everything else ancient that may be available."

"That is before I found the perfect place to swim. I have never known anywhere as lovely as it is here. The sea is exactly right as it really ought to be, but usually one is disappointed."

"I am glad it pleases you, Malva. In which case we had better now go and say 'good morning' to the waves as tomorrow we will not be able to do so."

"I am sure they will miss us," Malva giggled.

They swam most of the day racing each other until it was too hot and then they were lying in the water where it was shallow and talking of what they had seen yesterday.

Royden was very careful not to tell her what she would be seeing tomorrow.

Although she tried very hard to tempt him into an explanation, he shook his head.

"I want it to be a surprise," he insisted. "Actually, if you think about it, we have had very few surprises on this trip so far."

"That is unkind," Malva said. "I have had masses of surprises, especially Gibraltar which was more exciting than I expected it to be. To me this place is absolutely perfect – very close to my ideal of a Heaven on earth."

She thought as she spoke that she would be very sorry to leave.

Somehow it would be a mistake to go back to the world outside instead of living in this quiet little bay where there were no disturbances and nothing was said or heard that might upset or irritate them.

She wanted to stay with Royden for much longer.

She told herself, although she did not tell him, that she found him far more interesting and intriguing than any building or museum could be.

'Perhaps,' she reflected, 'he finds me rather boring and that is why he is looking forward to moving on.'

She enjoyed the conversation they had at luncheon.

And at dinner they had a long argument over what was the best collection of classic pictures to be found in the different countries of the world.

As she had read so much about art and Royden had seen so many pictures on his trips, their conversation was spirited.

At the same time so intelligent that he thought it a shame that it was not all being written down so that others could learn from their experiences.

Finally it was time to go to bed.

He made the move earlier than usual, because he said he wanted to leave sharp at eight o'clock the following morning when the conveyance that he had been promised would hopefully then be waiting for them.

"I am terribly curious as to where we are going and what we are doing," Malva asserted. "Equally you are quite right that it will be a surprise and I must not spoil the moment when I gasp at what you are showing me."

Royden grinned.

"I know that you are trying to get me to give you some little hint of what it is," he said, "but I refuse to be drawn out, so please go to bed and don't forget to be ready to leave immediately we have finished breakfast."

Malva walked to the door.

Then she turned back.

"I still think that today is the most delightful day I have ever spent and if only I could give this bay a present as a token of gratitude of what it has meant to me, I should be very glad to do so."

Royden laughed as she ran up the companionway towards her bedroom.

She climbed into bed and because she felt so happy she fell asleep almost at once.

She dreamt that once again she was lying in the shimmering waves and the sunshine was turning the whole world into a Fairyland.

*

She woke with a start because she heard a sound.

At first she did not recognise what it was.

Then she was aware that it was something beating or scratching at the porthole.

She rose from her bed and crossed the cabin to pull back the curtain.

Then she saw in the light from the moon that a bird was caught in some way at her cabin window.

It was trying in vain to escape.

She reached out, but the bird was at the part of the porthole that did not open.

She was unable to reach it, but she could see that it was caught by one leg although she was not certain what it was trapped by.

She stretched out as far as she could.

But it was impossible for her arm to pass the open porthole.

She now realised that to release the bird she must go up onto the deck above.

She put on her dressing gown and her soft slippers and found a pair of scissors in her drawer and with these she would cut away what was keeping the bird a prisoner.

As Malva opened the door of her cabin, she then hesitated for a moment wondering whether she should ask Royden to release the trapped bird instead of going on deck herself.

Then she told herself that he would be fast asleep and it would be unnecessary to wake him, especially as she herself was now so awake.

She moved slowly towards the companionway and walked out on deck without making a sound.

There was, she knew, usually a seaman on duty, but she had suspected long ago that when they were in Port he slept because it was so quiet.

Only when they were in a Port like Gibraltar did he make his rounds dutifully and stayed awake all through the night.

Her cabin was halfway along the deck and she had no difficulty in finding it from above and then leant over the rail.

She saw the bird fluttering frantically beneath her.

As she looked down, she could see that its leg was attached quite firmly to the side of the porthole.

She knelt down and bent forward to cut him loose with her pair of scissors.

As she did so, a heavy cloth was thrown over her head and she was lifted up from the deck.

A strong man was holding her in his arms.

She wanted to scream and tried to do so.

But the cloth was thrust into her mouth while it was open.

Try as she could she was unable to make a sound.

Then she was lifted up into the air and she thought for a moment that she was being flung into the sea.

Then she was aware that another man was holding her tightly.

As he lowered her, a third man held her firmly against him.

Next she was aware that they were in a boat and being rowed towards the shore.

She tried to scream again, but it was impossible to do so because the thick cover which had been thrown over her head prevented her from closing her lips.

Try as she may, no sound came out.

In fact there was no sound at all, only the lap of the water as the rowing boat slid through it.

Then the soft crunch as it came up on the beach.

One of the men picked her up in his arms.

She knew that she was being carried up the rough path that she and Royden had used which was the only way of entering the bay.

Then she was unceremoniously thrust into the back of a carriage which she thought must be enclosed.

Two of the men climbed in beside her and the door was shut.

There was a slight pause before the horses drawing it started off.

Malva guessed that there were two horses and they were certainly being driven very swiftly.

At first it was very rough and uneven so that the carriage swayed and bumped over the stony ground.

Then they were on what she supposed was sand and the carriage was moving even more swiftly.

Now the ride was smoother with only occasional bumps.

It was with increasing horror that she realised she was being kidnapped.

She could only imagine it was somehow connected with the Vizier they had visited the day before yesterday.

'How could he do such a thing?' she asked herself. 'And why?'

There was no answer to this and she realised that there was nothing she could do.

The heavy rough material covering her head also covered her arms.

Although she tried to move, it was quite impossible as there were two men sitting either side of her.

She was crushed between them and she recognised that she was completely helpless and it was no use trying to move or release herself in any way.

The horses were travelling swiftly and she guessed that the man in front was using his whip liberally to keep up the speed.

She wanted to cry out.

She wanted to ask where they were taking her.

But it was impossible to do anything but fight for her breath because of the heaviness of the material that covered her.

She was frightened, desperately frightened.

At the same time she told herself that she had to keep herself calm enough to argue with her captors when she learnt who they were and what they wanted of her.

It had taken her and Royden over an hour-and-a-half to reach the Vizier's Palace the day before yesterday.

But now, if that was where they were taking her and she had a very strong suspicion that it was, the horses stopped outside what she was sure was a gate.

Then they were moving more slowly down, as she suspected, the lane that led to the front door of the Palace, although she was not sure that was where she was being taken and if so why and for what reason.

Surely the Vizier was not holding her captive for money.

How could he dare to offend a visitor to his part of the world by taking her prisoner?

'It must be someone else,' she thought wildly.

Yet at the same time she remembered that both she and Royden had disliked the Vizier.

There had been something about him which she felt was unpleasant.

Even so to insult an innocent visitor to his country, even though he did not realise that Royden was of any

Social importance, would be to create a scandal that would certainly be taken up by the British Ambassador.

It could even cause a major international furore that would prevent other people from visiting this country.

The horses came to a standstill and now the men beside her lifted her out of the carriage.

But instead of putting her down onto the ground, as she expected, they then carried her between them for what seemed a long way.

She was sure that now they were in a room perhaps the grand one she had seen the day before yesterday with the elaborate mosaic floor.

Again she was only guessing.

Then she heard a door open.

The next moment she was put down almost roughly on a couch or a bed.

For the first time one of the men who was carrying her spoke.

He was addressing someone else.

Although she could not understand what the man was saying she felt that he must be telling whoever was listening that he had brought back the woman he had been sent to kidnap – and here she was.

Then Malva lay gasping for breath because it had been hard to breathe while she was being carried from the carriage to where she was now.

The heavy material which covered her completely was moved slowly off her.

She now found herself looking at two women, who were very much like those she had seen yesterday and were dressed in the same manner.

"What is happening? And where am I?" she asked in French.

To her relief one of them replied to her in the same language.

"You are here in the house of His Excellency, the Vizier."

"I thought it was where I was," Malva exclaimed. "But please tell me why have I been brought here in such an extraordinary manner?"

"The Vizier will tell you that himself," the woman replied.

Her French seemed somewhat limited.

Then she turned and spoke to the other woman in another language, which must have been Arabic.

She went away.

Then Malva sat up, smoothing back her hair from her face and trying to breathe naturally although it was a tremendous effort.

A few minutes later the woman who had left the room came back with a tray on which there was a glass of what looked like wine.

She handed it to Malva, who took it and sipped what she thought was a strange but rather sweet wine.

She felt relief from the dryness of her mouth.

"Drink it all and you will feel better," one of the women said.

Because her throat was feeling parched and she was finding it difficult to express herself, Malva did as she was told.

Then, as she finished the glass, she realised that she had been drugged.

Even as her eyes closed and she was aware that she was falling backwards, it was much too late to do anything about it.

*

It must have been many hours later when Malva opened her eyes because the sun was streaming in through a long pointed window.

She was sure that she must have been unconscious for several hours.

As she looked round the room, she was trying to remember why she was there and what had happened.

Then she realised that she was wearing her dressing gown and all that had happened last night came flooding back to her.

The room she had been taken into was beautifully decorated like the rest of the Palace and the bed she was lying on had a silk embroidered cover.

At the same time she had been taken forcibly away from the yacht and she could only lie there and wonder what Royden was doing about it and if he would guess what had happened to her.

'He might think I have drowned accidentally,' she thought. 'In which case he will go away and I will never see him or home again.'

Then she told herself he would be aware that she had left her bed.

He would be intelligent enough to realise that her dressing gown was missing whilst her bathing dress was where she had left it, hung over the wash basin so that it should dry.

'Save me! *Save me!*' she tried to cry out to him.

She wondered if he would know how frightened she was and how it was a desperate situation that it was impossible for her to escape from.

She remembered only too well the number of men and women who were waiting on the Vizier.

And there would indeed be no escape for anyone His Excellency wished to keep prisoner in his Palace.

'What can I do? What *can* I do?' she asked herself again and again.

But there was no answer.

All she could think of was how cleverly they had spirited her away, having lured her on deck by tying a bird against her porthole.

Now, as she lay back against the soft cushions, she was aware that the heavy material in which she had been kidnapped had vanished.

After she was drugged one of the women must have put a silk covering over her.

She still felt very dizzy and it was difficult to think clearly because of the drug.

She kicked herself for having been so stupid as to drink it just because her mouth was dry from lack of air.

Now she wondered what she could do and how it seemed almost impossible for her ever to reach Royden or let him know where she was.

'How dare the Vizier do anything so disgraceful as to capture a British woman and make her his prisoner?' she asked herself.

He probably thought they were French and would not be aware that he was insulting a country as important as England.

'I must keep my head and think what I can do and what I can say,' she told herself.

Then, as the drug was still making her feel faint and it was impossible to think, she closed her eyes and fell asleep.

When she awoke, she knew instinctively that it was much later in the day.

There was a woman sitting just inside the door and apparently watching her.

As her eyes opened, she turned her head first one way and then the other and made an effort to sit up.

The woman then hurried out of the room and Malva thought that she had gone to fetch the older woman.

In this she was right.

The two women who had been in the room when she had arrived came hurrying back in.

"You feel better? You like something to eat?" the first woman to enter the room asked her.

"I would like a drink of water, clear, clean water," Malva answered in French, "and with no drug in it."

The woman laughed.

"You sleep and sleep always good when one is tired or frightened."

"What I want to know," Malva said, sitting up and trying to speak firmly, "is why I am here and why I have been taken prisoner in this most unpleasant and offensive manner."

The two women looked at each other.

One shrugged her shoulders.

"His Excellency tell you later what you ask," she said. "Now when you have eaten, we will help dress you."

Although she was very frightened, Malva did not want the women to know this.

She therefore ate a little of the food they offered her.

She drank the clear water which they had told her had come from a spring that was pure and good for those who drank it.

She examined the water very carefully before she put it to her lips and she was sure that they were telling her the truth and, as she was very thirsty, she drank a glassful and felt better for doing so.

She was too scared, although she was determined not to show it, to want anything to eat.

The fruit they had brought her was, she was certain, safe to eat and so she ate a piece of plum and felt better still.

The moment she finished eating the food was taken away.

Then clothes were brought for her to wear.

They were naturally Eastern dress but attractive and colourful and were covered with shining jewels.

She sat down and one of the women brushed and combed her hair until it looked as striking as if she had done it herself.

Then at last there was a knock on the door and an order was given by one of the white-robed servants.

She could not understand what he had said, but she thought that the women were first of all surprised.

They chatted amongst themselves in low voices as if they were talking about something strange and unusual that had happened.

Because the day was drawing on and she could now think clearly, Malva was becoming increasingly concerned of what might happen when she met the Vizier.

She had the idea, in fact she was sure, that he had kidnapped her for some secret reason that she could not fathom out.

She could only tremble and pray to God fervently that somehow Royden would save her from whatever fate was to be hers.

She had not read a good number of books about the East without realising that a fair-haired woman was very attractive to men who were always surrounded by women with dark hair.

She also knew that someone as prominent as the Vizier would have numerous concubines at his disposal.

If she was honest, she was sensible enough to be aware that this was the reason why she had been brought to the Palace.

'Rather than become one of his concubines,' she thought, 'I would rather die.'

Then she wondered how it would be possible to kill herself without a proper weapon to do it with.

The women dressing her were fussing over her for what she suspected was an ominous reason.

They brought a collection of jewels to put round her neck and there were bracelets for her wrists and jewels to place in her hair.

When they had finished, they looked at her with pride.

Then one of them said,

"You are very beautiful, pretty lady. Vizier will think so and you be very grateful to His Excellency."

Malva stared at her.

Then she realised that this was the reason she had been taken prisoner.

The Vizier obviously wanted a fair-haired woman in his harem.

And that was why he had looked at her in such a strange and intrusive way when they had first met.

She wanted to scream, to run out of the room and try to escape from the Palace, but she knew that whatever happened she must keep her head and appear calm.

The women were attaching jewels to her ankles and to her feet.

Now they walked over to the door and there was a whispered conversation outside.

When they came back, one of the women said,

"His Excellency is waiting for you. You come with me."

The two women drew her through the door.

It was then she recognised one of the magnificent rooms they had passed through before.

She was aware that, at the far end of it, the Vizier was sitting at a table.

Because there was nothing else she could do, she walked with the women across the room.

She knew from the way they moved that they were in point of fact showing her off as if they had performed some clever feat in dressing her as they had.

As they then sank to the ground with bowed heads before the Vizier, Malva stood up holding her head high and regarded him defiantly.

The Vizier looked her up and down in a manner that she felt was not only degrading but distasteful.

Then he said in French,

"You may kneel down while I tell you why I have brought you here."

There was a pause before Malva retorted,

"I do *not* kneel, except to my God."

As she was speaking, she noticed at once that the two women stiffened.

The Vizier stared at her as if he was surprised.

"I should be most grateful," Malva said, "if Your Excellency will tell me why I have been brought here. You must be aware that my brother will be looking for me and will be extremely annoyed that I have been smuggled away from his yacht."

She was speaking in French but slowly and with a tremendous effort, proudly hoping that the Vizier would have no idea that her heart was pounding with fear.

For a moment he did not speak.

Then he said,

"Because you are French you may sit down at my table."

There was a cushion at the side of the table.

Malva moved to it slowly, sitting down in a manner which she thought would tell him without words that she was defiant and not afraid of him.

At the same time her heart was still thumping in her breast.

It was difficult for her to speak slowly and in a dignified manner.

The two women, who were still kneeling in front of the Vizier, peeped at her with puzzled eyes.

"My brother," Malva said again, "will now be out looking for me."

"But then he will not find you," the Vizier replied, "because I am now giving you the privilege of being in my harem."

"I cannot understand why you should expect me to be pleased at this happening to me," she countered. "You must be aware that until I marry I belong to my brother. Any request for ownership should be made to him."

"You are someone I definitely will appreciate," the Vizier went on, "because golden-haired women are not easy to find."

"My brother will doubtless bring in the Police to search for me," Malva answered breathlessly, "as well as notifying the Ambassador that I am missing."

She thought as she spoke there was just a flicker of surprise on the Vizier's face as if he was not aware that the Frenchman who had visited him was of any particular rank, except, of course, that he was rich enough to own a yacht.

Although she was sitting at the Vizier's table and he had food on a plate in front of him, she was offered nothing, not even some wine to drink.

The two women who had brought her were still kneeling on the floor.

"You are young, you are beautiful and you are fair-haired," the Vizier said slowly, as if he was convincing himself. "And I am very delighted to have you."

"I have no wish to belong to you," Malva said, "and I can only warn you that the trouble you have caused in kidnapping me will not only be the talk of this Continent but also in France when they learn of it."

She was speaking proudly and her head was held high.

Equally it was hard to say the words even when they came to her mind.

She was also aware that while she was clasping her hands together her fingers were trembling.

Then, as she finished speaking, she was aware that the Vizier was frowning.

He had been holding a glass of wine in his hand and now he put it down.

Clenching his fingers he brought his fist down hard on the table.

"You will do as I tell you!" he shouted angrily.

The words came tumbling from his lips.

"You are my prisoner and you belong to me. I don't want to hear any more of your rudeness."

His voice seemed to echo round the room.

As he finished speaking, there was absolute silence as if the furniture in the room as well as the women and servants listening were intimidated by the Vizier's anger.

Malva drew in her breath.

She knew that she was banging her head against a closed door.

However much she had defied him, she was in the Vizier's power.

With a tremendous effort she managed to reply,

"If you are brave enough to break all the rules of hospitality and to defy the French Government who will be very shocked by this, there is nothing more I can say."

For a moment the Vizier just glared at her.

Then he said,

"You are not important enough for the French to make trouble. France is full of beautiful women and if one is lost in the desert who will count her footsteps."

"My brother is a very influential man in business," Malva managed to reply. "He has also travelled a great deal and is well known in very many countries, especially in England. Her Majesty, Queen Victoria, would be really horrified at my being taken prisoner by you."

She spoke slowly and with a dignity that made the Vizier stare at her almost in astonishment.

"You say your brother is important," he said after a pause. "Why should I believe that? He is just Monsieur, he has no title. All the French who are important have a title."

With a great effort Malva gave a little laugh.

"But, of course, you would not understand that if my brother uses his title and he does have one, wherever we go we are given lavish luncheon and dinner parties. We have to waste our time, when we want to be alone resting, in attending many functions and meeting numerous people we have no particular interest in."

The Vizier stared at her.

"I don't believe you," he snapped.

"Then why should you when all we wish for is to be anonymous?" she replied. "We want to enjoy a holiday without the pomp and ceremony which we have to endure all the time."

She saw that the Vizier was listening and she went on,

"I am warning you that there will be a tremendous uproar when it is found that I am missing. It will not be difficult for my brother to guess that you are the thief who has stolen me away from him."

"Nonsense! All lies! You are not telling me the truth," the Vizier stormed.

His words seemed to echo and re-echo around the room.

Malva was aware that the two women kneeling in front of him had lowered their heads with fear.

The servants, who had left the room when she first came in, now were joined by others and were peeping in through the door as if they could hardly believe the noise they were hearing.

Then unexpectedly a door near to where the Vizier was sitting was flung open.

A servant announced,

"A visitor, Your Excellency, from His Highness the Sultan has just arrived."

Every head in the room was turned to the door.

A man came in dressed in the ceremonial robes of an Eastern Potentate.

On his head he was wearing a cap glittering with jewels. At his waist there was a long bejewelled dagger that proclaimed his rank even more than the medals which were round his neck.

His hair, or what could be seen of it, was very dark and his moustache, which curled over the sides of his lips, was black and gave the impression of being greasy.

He advanced slowly towards the Vizier, who rose to his feet.

CHAPTER SEVEN

"I come," the visitor said in a deep gravelly voice, "from his Highness the Sultan to ask of Your Excellency a very great favour."

The Vizier looked at him in surprise.

Then he said,

"You have not told me who you are."

"I am the Chief Eunuch of His Highness's harem."

Listening Malva guessed that he must be the Head and Controller of it.

And she wondered why this ornate man should be calling at this hour on the Vizier.

But she was so terrified of her own position that she could think of nothing else except that the newcomer broke the rising tension, at least for a time, between herself and the Vizier.

As if he realised that he was not quite as important as he thought he was at first, the Vizier then sat down and indicated with a snap of his fingers that the servants should bring the newcomer a chair.

They hurried to do so.

But the Chief Eunuch stood where he was, saying,

"I am asking in the Sultan's name, if you will let me have for this evening's party, which he is giving to a number of distinguished visitors, the fair-haired concubine you have just taken into your Palace."

The Vizier stared at him.

Then he asked,

"How can His Highness know of such things? She only arrived today."

The Chief Eunuch laughed.

"Stories, as Your Excellency well knows, travel in the desert on the wind. When my Master heard of your discovery, he was very anxious for her to take part in the parade that is taking place tonight for his visitors. All his concubines are splendidly dressed and will take part. But, alas, there is not one of them with fair golden hair."

The Vizier laughed.

"So for once I have more concubines here at my Palace than His Highness has at his!"

"He promises to return her tomorrow," the Eunuch said. "But it will make all the difference if he can show her tonight amongst his own collection which you are well aware is very much envied."

The Vizier laughed again.

There was silence until the Chief Eunuch added,

"Time is getting on. Although I have fast horses, it is quite a way, as Your Excellency knows, to the Sultan's Palace."

The Vizier was biting one of his finger nails and looking at Malva.

She felt herself tremble at the aggressive expression in his eyes.

Then the Chief Eunuch said,

"I beg of you don't make me return to His Highness with an empty carriage. You know how demanding he can be and he has set his heart on showing his friends that there is one golden concubine amongst all the dark ones."

The Vizier gave a laugh that had no humour in it.

"Very well then, but she is to remain untouched and returned to me tomorrow. Is that understood?"

"I feel sure that looking at the concubine of whom you are speaking, that His Highness will understand your feelings and your wish will be respected. She will be back with you by this time tomorrow evening."

"And untouched and unharmed?" the Vizier snarled questioningly.

The Chief Eunuch bowed as he said,

"You are very very generous, Your Excellency, and it is something His Highness will not forget."

The Vizier snapped his fingers.

Those servants, who had been listening attentively to what was being said, hurried to bring a wrap across the room. It was of a deep shade of pink.

As Malva knew that it was for her, she rose from her seat and let them envelop her in the silk wrap.

There was a heavy silence as the servants covered her completely, leaving only her face showing.

They must have felt her trembling as their hands passed over her.

As the Chief Eunuch bowed again to the Vizier, he said,

"Your gracious gift and your acquiescence to His Highness's demand will not be forgotten."

"I would indeed hope not," the Vizier replied, "for you have spoilt my evening and my night."

The Eunuch gave a laugh and added,

"You know, as well as I do, Your Excellency, that whatever we may feel the Sultan must always be obeyed at whatever inconvenience we ourselves suffer personally."

"There you speak the truth," the Vizier answered. "Be quite certain that this precious belonging of mine is returned to me uninjured."

"To hear is to obey," the Chief Eunuch said.

Having bowed his head politely, he walked to the door without even a glance at the wrapped figure behind him.

Because it was difficult to walk, two men picked up Malva and carried her.

As they went outside, the sun was setting and it was still not dark.

There was an exceedingly large and fine-looking carriage drawn by four horses waiting outside.

The drivers were wearing fantastic livery and the carriage itself was also decorated in gaudy colours.

It was not surprising that a crowd of people from the village were staring at it with admiration.

When the Chief Eunuch appeared in all his finery, they cheered him and clapped their hands.

They also looked with surprise and astonishment at the fact that he was taking away one of the women who they knew belonged to the Vizier.

The Chief Eunuch climbed into the carriage first.

The two men who had carried Malva placed her on the back seat beside him.

When he gave them money for their attention, they thanked him profusely before the doors were closed and the man driving the four horses leapt into the driving seat.

The carriage began to move.

It was only as they drove on out of earshot of the Palace that the Chief Eunuch pulled off his moustache and said in a very different voice from the one that he had used when addressing the Vizier,

"Now, my darling, *you are free!*"

For a moment Malva could only stare at him.

Then in the light from the sky she saw, although it seemed incredible, that it was Royden who was sitting next to her.

She gave a cry of astonishment.

Then, throwing herself against him, she burst into tears.

"It is *you*, it is you." she cried. "I thought I would never see you again. How could you be so clever? I could not look at you because I was so afraid of what you were saying."

Royden pulled off his jewelled cap and his wig and flung them on the floor and then he drew her close to him.

"It is all right, my precious," he said. "It has been a horrid experience, I know, but I saved you and this will never happen again."

Because she was still crying against his shoulder, Malva did not look up.

At the same time, as he pushed away the silk wrap, his arms went round her and she hid her face closer against his neck.

"I thought that – you would never – be able to save me," she sobbed.

"How could I do anything else? If I had had to burn down the Palace and kill the Vizier myself, I would have done so. But, as it is you are free, my darling."

"Is it really true – I am safe?" Malva asked.

She looked up wide-eyed at him as she spoke.

Then his lips came down on hers.

He kissed her at first very gently and then more passionately.

His arms tightened around her until it was difficult for her to breathe.

Only when they had travelled for quite some way did Royden raise his head to say,

"Did you really think I would leave you with that devil?"

"But – how did you find me?" she managed to ask.

"Fortunately a seaman who was on duty and who, of course, had been asleep, saw you at the last moment as they carried you up the pathway. He roused me, but I was too late. But I knew what had happened and cursed myself because I was so stupid in taking you to see a man who would appreciate the fact that you had fair hair in a land where all the women are dark."

"But you saved me – and I was trying to think of how I could – kill myself before he touched me."

Royden's arms tightened.

"No man will ever touch you except me and I will kill anyone who tries to do so," he asserted fervently.

He kissed her again before she could reply.

Because his kisses were a force that she felt moved her heart from her breast into his, she could for a moment think of nothing.

Now the horses were moving over the rather bumpy stones.

It was Heaven, she thought, to be close in Royden's arms and to feel that she was safe at last.

Safe from the dreadful Vizier and the horror of what he intended for her.

As Royden raised his lips from hers, he exclaimed,

"You are mine! Mine, my precious darling Malva, and no other man will ever touch you."

As if she had suddenly woken to what was really happening to her, Malva stared at him although it was hard to see his face clearly.

In a whisper he could hardly hear, she asked him,

"Are you saying that you love me?"

"I love you with all my heart and soul," he replied, "and it is something I thought would never happen to me. When I knew that devil had taken you from me, I realised at once that I was losing everything that had ever mattered to me."

"You really love me?" Malva asked him again in an incredulous whisper.

"I have loved you for a long time," he answered, "but I fought against it because you had been so positive in saying that you could never love me."

"I loved you too," Malva murmured, "but I would not even admit it to myself, thinking that when we returned home to England you would leave me and I would never be able to love anyone else for the rest of my life."

Royden smiled.

"I know exactly what you were feeling and I was feeling the same. That was why I kept complete control of myself until I realised that you had been stolen from me."

He paused before he went on,

"Then I realised I was losing the only thing which really mattered in my life. You are the only person I have ever really loved with my whole heart."

Malva gave a little cry.

"Oh, my darling, wonderful Royden. Is that really – true?"

"I swear to you that all the nonsense I talked about never loving anyone in my life and never getting married had vanished from me before we reached Gibraltar. These last days I have been fighting against my feelings because I believed that you did not care for me."

"I love you, I love you, "Malva whispered. "When they took me away and I knew that horrible Vizier would try to make me his, I was wondering just – how I could kill myself before he could touch me."

Royden's arms closed round her.

"You are not going to die, my darling," he said. "We are going to live together and be so happy that no one will ever dare lay a finger on you."

There was a tremor in his voice which told her how much he had suffered when he realised that she had been taken from him.

"I love you, I love you with all my heart," she said. "But I thought, as you had sworn never to marry anyone, that you would never love me."

"I was talking absolute nonsense," Royden replied. "No, my precious one, we are going to get married so that wearing my ring no man will dare touch you. If he does, as I have already said, I will kill him."

Malva hid her face against his shoulder.

"I am so happy," she exclaimed, "after being so frightened, that I feel I must be living in a Divine dream."

"We will dream on together. I am going to tell the Captain that, as soon as we are on board, he is to move the yacht down to Dakar."

"Shall we be safe there?" Malva asked nervously.

"We will not stay there for more than one day," he replied. "And, as soon as we are married, we will leave."

"*Married*!" Malva exclaimed.

"You don't think I could live with you now and not make you, as I long to do, my wife," he said. "We both know that we have come away pretending to be married so as to avoid our relations nagging at us."

He paused before he carried on,

"But now they will think that we have been very clever because when we return home we will be already married and there will be no wedding reception waiting for us. Only a small party or maybe a ball to celebrate our homecoming, so that then our marriage could be officially announced without anyone knowing exactly where it took place."

There was silence for a moment.

Then Malva asked him,

"Are we really to be married in Dakar?"

"I cannot think of a better place where no one will be that interested and the Priest will know our names but not our titles," Royden answered.

Malva moved a little closer to him.

"You think of – everything," she sighed.

"I think of you," he replied, "as I do now and will always do in the future. But we will leave here tomorrow and have our honeymoon in other parts of the world where golden-haired women are not so valuable!"

Malva laughed.

"You make it sound so funny, but I was absolutely petrified."

"Of course you were, my precious darling," Royden sympathised. "If I had not been able to rescue you, I think I would have killed that ghastly Vizier."

"I still cannot believe it that you deceived him so cleverly," Malva said. "Where did this marvellous carriage come from and your clothes? I only looked at you once, but I had no idea that it was you."

"You have to thank the friend of mine who runs the Museum of Dakar. He lent me the clothes, the covering on the carriage and knew exactly where I could hire the horses and their attendants. He is called Valerian Fitzgerald and he is a delightful fellow."

Royden laughed as he went on,

"As I pretended to come from the Sultan, I had to look particularly impressive and I hope you admired my clothes and my extravagant jewels, which were all exhibits from the Museum."

Now it was Malva's turn to laugh.

"How could you be so clever? I just cannot think of anyone else who could possibly, and in such a short time, conceive of anything so spectacular to deceive the Vizier with."

"I am only sorry I cannot see his anger when you are not returned to him tomorrow morning," Royden said, "and he realises that he has been taken for a mug."

Malva did not have to answer him, because at that moment they arrived at the bay and she could see a number of the crew waiting for them on top of the cliff.

She looked out of the carriage window and waved.

When they could see that she was there, the men all cheered knowing that Royden had left in disguise to rescue her.

The men who had driven the horses were delighted with the money Royden gave them and then they drove off waving to the seamen who cheered as they went.

Very soon when everyone was back on the yacht, the Captain had his orders to sail away and the engines began to turn.

Malva went straight to her cabin.

And when Royden joined her a little later, she had pulled off the gown she had been dressed in and was now wearing only her dressing gown which was of a soft blue that accentuated the gold of her hair.

Later when Royden came into the cabin, he carried a bottle of champagne in his hand,

"I am bringing you a drink, my darling," he said. "I think that we not only both deserve it but we must drink to the future when I swear that you will never be frightened again."

"I was very very scared," Malva whispered. "But you saved me and no one could have been more wonderful than you."

She looked up at him with an expression in her eyes that he had always wanted to see in a woman.

This was real love.

The love he had been seeking all his life, but had never found until now.

For a moment he could only stand gazing at her.

Then very gently his lips found hers.

"I love you, I adore you," he breathed, "and I had no idea that love was so wonderful."

Malva gave a laugh and then put her arms round his neck.

"I talked such nonsense when I said I would never marry," she sighed.

Royden's arms tightened round her.

"You are incredibly beautiful, my darling one," he murmured.

He kissed her.

Then they remembered the champagne and they sat down on the bed to drink each other's health.

"They drugged me when I arrived at the Palace," Malva told him. "I slept for several hours so it was only when I finally woke that I became so very frightened and wondered desperately how I could kill myself."

"Forget it, darling. We are not going to think about it again. Only about the future and how happy we will be when we get back to The Towers and make it the most perfect place for our children."

Malva blushed and he added,

"Does that make you feel shy, my darling one? I know I talked rubbish when I said I did not want to be married. I want a wife and I want an heir to follow me and a fair-haired daughter as beautiful as you and perhaps two or three sons to play cricket with and to ride my best horses on the Racecourse."

Malva gave a little cry.

"You go too fast! How can we possibly have all that so quickly?"

"There is no hurry," he answered. "But it is what I want and look forward to in the future and I want you, my precious one, to look forward to it too."

"All I want," Malva replied, "is to be with you and to talk to you and to love you even more than I love you now, which I think is impossible!"

"I thought when I first realised that I was falling in love with you," Royden said, "that it might be impossible to make you love me. You were so very positive in saying that you would never marry anyone and I believed you."

"I believed myself, which was very silly of me. I might have known that it would be impossible for anyone to be with someone as clever, charming and amusing as you and not fall in love with him."

"That is just what I was going to say about you," Royden told her. "It's going to be difficult to find enough words to tell you just how magnificent you are."

As he spoke, he put his arms around her.

Then he said,

"I am going to leave you now, my darling, but I do so want you to enjoy every moment of our wedding day which is tomorrow."

"Can we really be married so quickly without any difficulty?" Malva asked.

"I happen to know a Priest who I met in Dakar. Because he was tremendously interested in the research I was doing at the time, we met several times and I know that he would oblige me by marrying us secretly and then making it certain that the news does not reach the English Press until we ourselves announce it on our return."

"That is one fence we have jumped safely," Malva said. "I want very much to be your wife whatever you may be disguised as and however long we have to remain in hiding."

"We are going to hide until we can announce our marriage without shocking the Queen. But, as it will be our honeymoon, I am going to take you to all the beautiful places I have visited in the past and I know they will seem even more glorious to me because you are with me."

"Where shall we start?" Malva asked eagerly. "I want to get away from here and not see an Arab again for a very long time!"

"As I want you to feel completely and absolutely safe, I think we will visit Greece. It has always been the land of love and I will tell you on Mount Olympus that to me you will always be the Goddess of Love."

Malva gave a cry.

"Oh, I would so love that. I would adore to see Olympus and, of course, the other parts of Greece I have read so much about. To me you will always be the King of Love – Apollo."

Royden laughed.

"I will not attempt the impossible, but I do promise you, my darling, that I will love you for the rest of my life and I know instinctively that our love will grow and grow year by year as we become older and wiser."

Then before she could answer, he was kissing her.

*

The next day they woke up to find that they were approaching Dakar.

Royden insisted that they went first to the Museum.

All the costumes he had borrowed from his friend, Valerian, especially the jewellery, had been very carefully packed by his valet.

They hired a carriage and set off for the Museum which Malva found fascinating and Royden's friend was charming.

"I know without you telling me that you have been successful," Valerian said as they appeared.

"All of it thanks to you," Royden replied, "and the wonderful advice you gave me."

He turned to Malva as he said,

"May I introduce my future wife, who is as anxious as I am to thank you for all you have done to help us?"

"Your future wife!" Valerian exclaimed. "Now I can see why you were so anxious not to let anything so sublime and so beautiful be stolen from you.

"Now you are making me blush," Malva responded. "But thank you so very much for all you did for Royden and for me."

"I am delighted to know that he was successful," he replied, "and I hope you admired him when he was dressed in those flamboyant clothes that have not been worn by anyone for almost a century."

"They have been packed up carefully and nothing has been damaged," Royden assured him. "And you must certainly add to the book you are writing that even after being on show in your Museum for so long, they still had the power to make me successful as you said I would be in such a disguise."

"I am sure that they were so delighted to have the opportunity of showing themselves off on a human being rather than just being here in this building," Valerian said. "Even so it will add to the stories of the many artefacts that are here, some of which have caused the death of a great number of people. While others, like the clothes you wore last night, have saved someone as ethereal as the lady you tell me will be your future wife."

Malva felt that the way he was speaking was very endearing.

She thanked him profusely for helping Royden to deceive the Vizier.

"You must not talk about it," Valerian said, "or you will get me into trouble. When it is discovered that you were merely taking back what they had stolen from you, they will lose face and then the Vizier will be extremely angry at having been deceived."

"That is why we are leaving almost immediately," Royden replied. "I am hoping that I can somehow return the kindness you have given me in some practical manner."

"You can do that quite easily," Valerian said, "if you can send me something from England which is unique and will not be anything I could possibly find myself from any collection in this part of the world."

"I promise," Royden assured him, "that you will have either a painting or something really special from my collection at Hillingwood Towers."

Valerian Fitzgerald looked delighted.

When they shook hands, he said again,

"It has been a great pleasure and a great delight to see you, Royden, and you must not forget your promise as it will be something I will not only show to those who visit me but enjoy myself."

"I swear to you it will be the first thing Malva and I will do when we reach England, but we will not be back at home until the autumn."

"I think that I can just manage to wait that long," Valerian smiled with a twinkle in his eyes.

*

After they left him, Royden took Malva through the narrow streets and the poorer part of Dakar.

Situated close by the Port was a little Church that Malva thought was more likely to be used by seamen than anyone else.

It certainly seemed to fit in with the Port itself and she was not surprised when she entered to find that there were fishing nets suspended from the ceiling.

The Church was very old and must have been built before the Port itself was opened.

As they entered, they saw that kneeling in front of the altar there was a white-haired man.

They walked silently up the aisle until they reached him.

As he rose to his feet and turned round, he looked at Royden and gave a cry of delight.

"Royden, is it really you after all these years?" he asked.

"Yes, it is me, Father, and I have come here to ask you to perform a very special ceremony for me," Royden replied.

"What is that?" the Priest enquired.

"I wish to be married secretly and I have brought you my future wife knowing that you will be as kind and as welcoming to her as you have always been to me."

The Priest held out both his hands to Malva and said,

"I cannot imagine anything that I would enjoy more than marrying my dear Royden to someone as beautiful as you, my child."

Malva smiled and blushed a little.

"Thank you," she murmured. "Royden has told me how kind you have always been to him."

"He has been very good to me and we have often talked of his future," the Priest replied. "He has always told me that he would never marry anyone, but now I have seen you I know why he has changed his mind!"

Malva smiled.

"Thank you for the nice things you are saying and Royden will explain why we are being married secretly."

Royden told the Priest that it was because Malva was in mourning and Queen Victoria would insist on them waiting for far longer than they wished to do.

"If we can be married secretly," he said, "we can spend our honeymoon exploring exotic places that Malva has never seen and which I know she will enjoy as much as meeting you, Father."

"It will be a great joy and delight to me," the Priest said, "to marry you both and, of course, I will keep your secret as you have asked me until you are free to let Her Majesty appreciate that love is more important in life than anything else."

"That is exactly what we have found and what we believe," Royden agreed. "Therefore, Father, we would like to be married at once if it is possible for you to do so."

"I will go and put on my vestments. As it is to be a secret marriage, if you will close the door and bolt it, there will be no one here until the ceremony is over."

He walked to what was obviously the Vestry door as he added,

"I suggest you light all the candles on the altar and those at the side."

He disappeared through the Vestry door.

As Malva hurried down the aisle to close the door of the Church and lock it, Royden lit all the candles he could find.

The light from the candles made the small rather dark building seem even more attractive than it had been before.

As Malva knelt to pray, she was thinking of how many other people must have knelt and prayed here in this serene little Church and received comfort and blessings.

Wives, before their husbands had gone out to sea, praying that they would come back safely.

Perhaps the men themselves knowing the dangers that lay ahead had asked God's help to save and protect them.

She thought it was very typical of Royden to have made friends with a man who she realised at one glance was not only holy but had an exceptional personality which one seldom found anywhere.

'What I must pray for,' she thought to herself, 'is that I must be clever enough to keep Royden's love and make absolutely sure that he never regrets having given up the freedom he used to value so highly.'

The Priest came back in his vestments which were very old and beautifully embroidered with sacred images.

Then, as Royden knelt beside Malva, she knew that this was one of the most significant days of her whole life.

It was something that she would always remember.

The Marriage Service was short, but the Priest said it with such sincerity that Malva felt that every word was blessing them both.

When they left, they would have gained something new that had never been there before.

Something that came from God Himself and which now joined them with Him.

The prayers the Priest said over them made her feel that every blessing was pouring from him into them.

Because of the holiness that enveloped them, they would take with them for ever the eternal blessing and the nearness of God which he was giving them when he joined them together as man and wife.

When the Service was over, they rose from their knees.

Royden gave the Priest a large sum of money to go to the poor of the City.

"You have made both of us very happy, Father," he said. "I can only thank you from the very bottom of my heart."

"It has been one of the most delightful days of my life to unite you as man and wife," the Priest replied. "Of course you will always be in my prayers from now until I die."

It was impossible to think of anything else as they walked hand in hand out of the beautiful Church into the brilliant sunshine outside.

They stepped aboard the yacht, which was waiting for them at the other side of the Port.

As soon as they were on board, the engines began to turn.

As they went further out to sea, Malva knew that they were now leaving the desert for ever.

And she was quite certain that they would never come back.

*

They had luncheon on board.

Then because the heat from the sun had grown very strong and, as Royden said they were in the East and the East was always very hot at that time of day, they went into the Master cabin.

Malva was looking so happy and beautiful it would have been difficult for him not to kiss her while they were having luncheon.

As he took her in his arms, he sighed,

"I have been tortured for long enough and now I can kiss you as I really want to kiss you. I can tell you, my darling, in kisses rather than words how much you mean to me."

He kissed her until they were both breathless.

Then, slipping off the thin dress she was wearing, he carried her into the big bed.

As he joined her, she gazed at Royden and sighed,

"I thought, darling, this would never happen to me. Yet today when we were being married I knew that neither your life nor mine would be complete unless we had found and married the one we loved."

"It is what I have been searching for all my life," Royden said. "I think I only said I never intended to marry simply because I was always disillusioned sooner or later, perhaps bored is the right word, by the women I was with."

He smiled tenderly for a moment before he went on,

"But with you, my precious Malva, it is very very different. I love not only your beauty but your brains and every part of you that now belongs to me. That is what I have always wanted, but not been aware of until now. I know that I am the most fortunate man in the whole wide world."

Malva gave a little cry,

"That is what I want you to feel and I have been praying all the time we were being married that I would never disappoint you and we would find the love we have always longed for but pretended we did not want."

She gave a sigh before she added,

"But now we will cherish our wonderful love and it will increase day by day and year by year."

"That is what I want you to say and you have put it in far better words than I could," he replied.

Then he was kissing her, kissing her at first gently and then demandingly as if he was asking her to surrender herself completely to her.

When finally he made Malva his, she felt as if he carried her up into the sky and then the sun enveloped them until they were burning with the fire and wonder of it.

It was Love.

The Love they had both thought was impossible to find, the love which is part of God, which comes from God and would be theirs for all Eternity and beyond into an Infinity of happiness.